Historical Soil

By

J.B. Jeffrey

PublishAmerica
Baltimore

First printing

At the specific preference of the author, PublishAmerica allowed this work to remain exactly as the author intended, verbatim, without editorial input.

This book is a work of fiction. Names, characters, places, and incidents are products of the author's imagination or are used fictitiously. Any resemblance to actual events or locales or persons, living or dead, is entirely coincidental

ISBN: 1-4241-2977-X
PUBLISHED BY PUBLISHAMERICA, LLLP
www.publishamerica.com
Baltimore

Printed in the United States of America

Dedicated to
Austen

PREMATURE BURIAL

To die is natural; but the living death
Of those who waken into consciousness,
Though for a moment only, ay, or less,
To find a coffin stifling their last breath,
Surpasses every horror underneath
The sun of Heaven, and should surely check
Haste in the living to remove the wreck
Of what was just before, the soul's fair sheath,
How many have been smothered in their shroud!
How many have sustained this awful woe!
Humanity would shudder could we know
how many have cried to God in anguish loud,
Accusing those whose haste a wrong had wrought
Beyond the worst that ever devil thought.

Chapter One

Treatment rooms in doctor's offices are by and large undersized, cold and awkward places where patients are left to anticipate the outcomes of their medical testing. Crinkly white paper shields the examination table. It's the variety of paper that reacts wildly when the doctor is invasive and poking his way around your body. It's the kind of paper that rolls out onto the table from a dispenser below before the arrival of the next patient. All very sanitary. Prehistoric Readers Digest Magazines litter the small side table. How many times can you read about the demolition of the Berlin Wall? Not exactly current events but the magazines help kill the waiting time quite tolerably.

Dr. Ken Stratten removes a substantial medical file from a slot on the outside of the treatment room door then enters. Officer A. J. Benson is positioned on the sterile papered table in his underwear awaiting the results of weeks of comprehensive tests to establish the cause of his calamity.

"A.J. put your clothes on, you're done." chirps Stratten.

"What do you mean I'm done? You mean I'm done for good, like terminally done?" Benson says with a robust laugh.

"You're terminally stubborn perhaps, but not terminally ill otherwise." the doctor replies.

"You've been a detective for a long time A.J. You know bloody well what's wrong with you. I'm just the guy to confirm the diagnosis, that's all."

"OK doc, give me a break and cut the bullshit out here, I got bad guys on the streets here that need my attention." Benson barks.

"My prescription is that your criminal chasing days are over, at least for now. A. J., you have a serious condition called working yourself to fucking death. That's not the textbook definition mind you. The ulcer, the chronic upset stomach, the sharp pain in your gut is the result of the stressors in your life."

"What do you mean stressors? What the hell is that?"

"A stressor is anything that causes deterioration on your body's physical of mental resources. I believe the biggest contributing stressor in your life is your work. No! Correct that, I know bloody well that your work is your stressor."

"Bullshit brother, bullshit. You know what I've been up against in the last couple of years, what the fuck are you doing dressing it up as some medical fuck up?"

"Because it is now medical, probably always was. Your mind and body are in a state of chaos. This has happened to you before."

That being said, A.J. pulls his pressed white shirt off the hanger on the back of the door in an attempt to terminate his meeting with Dr. Stratten.

"Listen to me A. J." the Doctor continues "You were nearly assassinated last year. You went back to work too soon after your surgery. The D.A. was wrong to call you to testify so soon after your ordeal and as beautiful as your Chief of Detectives is, she erred in allowing you back in the saddle as soon as she did."

"Bullshit, ordeal my ass, I got shot, I'm a cop, it happens, too bad but it's part of the job." a now very defiant A.J. says.

"My brother, you have a condition called G.A.S." Stratten injects, "and not the kind that comes spurting out of your ass after a night on beer and Buffalo chicken wings either."

Annoyed at his step brother now, A. J. pulls his silk tie into place, the knot in perfect position, fastens his sleek leather belt around his waist and moves toward the door. The doctor moves in front of him to block the door.

"A. J. you are a sick man, and when I make my report to your superiors, they will see it the same way."

"You prick, would you do that to me? Really?"

"I have a medical obligation to you, but more than that, I have a brotherly obligation to you. Before our mother died, I promised her I would keep a close eye on you, at her urging I might add. Mother was very insistent on this A. J. I know that times were tough before I was born and that losing your father when you were a kid was traumatic to you. I suppose mother recognized the long term effect this might have on you. She knew how dedicated you are to your work and how undedicated you had become about other things in life."

"What kind of shit is this?"

"I don't have time for this family chat today alright. Do you want to listen to me now as your doctor or don't you care?" The doctor said with a final thrust of authority.

"Sum it up nice and tight here then."

"You have a condition that we call General Adaptation Syndrome, or GAS. You've heard these conditions also called Post Traumatic Stress Disorder haven't you?" questions the doctor.

"I guess, but I don't think that I…" he stutters

"Ongoing chronic stress results in physical and mental illness. Your shitty diet and abuse of alcohol has added to it." he said.

"OK, OK, old story, don't go there."

"Oh yes! We are going there whether you like it or not! You need to acknowledge you have PTSD before you can get any better. It's all relative, these medical conditions of yours. You need to take some time away from your job. You've got time coming don't you? Fucking Buffalo Police Department was here a hundred years before you enrolled, and they'll be there for a long time after you leave, so please, for our mother, take some time away. Your job will be there when you come back. I'm prescribing a treatment therapy for you immediately. Let's monitor how the drugs cure your ulcers and stomach irritation first.

"First?"

"You can't heal mentally if your guts are hurting you and you keep drinking to ease the pain."

"You are a complete prick you know." Says A. J.

"Thank you" the doctor retorts, quite uninterested at being chastised.

"I am prescribing a lengthy sabbatical for you. Take this time to heal, do some reading and get into shape. Travel, take up a hobby, but just keep away from job stress."

"Easy for you to say, I hate to sit and do nothing, you know that."

"Maybe I should schedule you for a hearing test! I'm not saying to sit at home watching the television for 24 hours. I'm telling you to find something to do to relax. Be productive by doing something else for a change."

A. J. has been dealt a heavy blow by his step brother, but he recognizes the truth when he hears it. He must now admit he is mentally unable to do his job, a job he loves and has always lived for. The job was always more important than other things in his life. Regrettably, these things are now are catching up with him fast.

A. J. readjusts his tie, checks the crease in his pants and pulls on his shoulder holster as moves toward the door.

It's been an awkward morning for both men. Both are experts at what they do, both enjoying demanding careers, one brother enjoying his job so much he pays no heed to the tragic consequences of being so dedicated.

"A. J., just take the time off now. I'll come by your place tonight after appointments and drop off the prescriptions for you with my recommendations. I'm also making a referral for you to see to Dr. Liberte.

"Who the fuck is that?"

"She's a Psychiatrist. Dr. Marisa Liberte. I've worked with her at Erie County Medical Centre for years. I want her to provide your employer with a report on your Post Traumatic Stress Disorder. That should free some time up for you away from the force."

"Yep, well, that should do it for my career too I would say. My career will be right in there with the Tidy-Bowl man" he grunts.

"This is a treatment plan for you, don't you understand? Without this plan of action, you will become more mentally unstable, accelerating and degrading your already vulnerable mental state. This mental instability will increase if not treated. You will begin to experience episodes that will handicap you mentally. It is a debilitating disease so I recommend you don't fuck with it."

"Bullshit."

"It's not bullshit. Your day to day functioning will be affected, you will become maladaptive. The disease will impair normal intellectual functioning, and might even prevent you from managing your day to day routine. You will become more dependent on alcohol and drugs, more than you are now, and your ability to reason will be diminished." Dr. Stratten says.

"Come by the house tonight then if you want to. Do you remember how to get there? You haven't been there for a long time. You still drink Canadian Club?" asks A. J.

"Yes, I still drink it. But I can drink it, my health is fine" The doctor said flatly as his brother leaves the office waving off any further dialogue.

Chapter Two

Witnessing the bodies of the two adults and two children fly around inside a car in a head on crash is a frightening site initially. After the first four or five medium speed impacts however, the reporters covering the story grow somewhat accustomed.

The photo-op afforded to the local television stations and print media is a twice yearly ritual which ties in nicely to the recently released Crash Test and Rollover Ratings from Buffalo Research and Innovation Centre.

The BRIC is a private company, founded by Brent Carl in the early 1980's. Carl's company receives a substantial amount of funding from the federal government to perform independent testing on new model motor vehicles.

Carl began his career in the car business in auto body repair. He attended a local community college and afterward apprenticed at a Buffalo GM dealer. After working his way to the position of Body Shop Manager, the flamboyant and well spoken Carl was often called upon to provide some quick quotes to the local television news telecasts when they reported on car crashes.

Buffalo has four local television stations, all affiliated with a major network. These stations are responsible to produce at least one half hour of local news programming per day. The major nets would pick up with their own news following the local dribble from Buffalo and Western New York State.

Carl's standard comments to the reporter at the scene of a crash would be on the subject of how he didn't think that a crash at such a low speed should result in so much damage to the vehicles or death of the cars occupants. Alternatively, he would comment on the fact that the sturdy structure of this vehicle saved the lives of the occupants. Every time there was a major vehicle crash, Carl's phone would ring at the dealership.

"Irv Feinstein here from News Centre 3." the voice on the other end said. "We need a couple of minutes on tonight's news about the safety rating on the new imported SUV's."

"Hi Carl, Sally Banks here from Channel 7, can you get back to me?"

"Carl, this is Kelly Richmond at Newscentre 2 here, I need some comments about the safety of the new Montage Van. I'm just dispatching a crew out to the I90 at Tonawanda. Seems there's another rollover with the new Montage. Can you meet our satellite truck out there? Can you get back to me?" he asks.

As more time was spent cooing with the local press on vehicle safety issues, less time was spent on managing the body shop. The owners of the dealership dealt the ace card to Brent and fired him just before his summer holidays.

Brent Carl became a household name of sorts from his exposure on local television news. He combined his personality status with his generous severance package and decided that consulting and research was going to be his new career. After all, everyone was calling him for his professional opinion, so why shouldn't he try to parlay that into some cold hard cash?

For several months Brent lobbied Federal Safety Administration executives on the virtues of an independent testing centre for the Western New York and Buffalo area. Buffalo was in a period of rebirth and regeneration at that time and Brent sold local, state and federal authorities on the plan.

Old buildings were being toppled, replaced by ultramodern cavities for business. New industry was being attracted to the region by all levels of government. New transit systems were being constructed. Things were looking good in Buffalo. Little was left of the old infrastructure as the new Buffalo emerged.

In due course and time, all levels of Government responded

positively and agreed that to have a vehicle testing centre like the one Brent Carl was proposing was perfect for this area. Buffalo was emerging as a high tech centre, shedding its past image as an industrial hub.

Federal, state and local funds came pouring into the project. Carl appointed himself king and ruler of the company to be called The Buffalo Research and Innovation Centre.

Futuristic technologies were soon installed into the brand new lakefront building housing the Buffalo Research and Innovation Centre. A team of experts were hand picked by Brent and the feds to operate the diagnostics that would soon be up and running to perform crash tests and rollover ratings for the major car companies. Agreements structured by the Federal Government were soon in place with all of the car companies selling vehicles in North America and Mexico.

These agreements covered the terms by which compensation would be paid to BRIC and included how and when new vehicles would be delivered to the new facility for testing.

New vehicles, hot off the assembly lines of car plants all over North America, Japan, Korea and Europe soon began arriving. Upon arrival, the car would be inspected, given a testing number and placed in a holding pattern in an adjacent warehouse until the testing was scheduled for that particular model.

The work was plentiful as car companies began producing what they would eventually term *The SUV*. Because Carl's facility housed the most modern testing equipment and staffed by the nations most respected names, car companies were anxious to have Buffalo Research and Innovation Centre do their testing. To have BRIC report on the safety of a particular vehicle bestowed instant credibility on the vehicle as far as safety was concerned. It was obligatory to have the local press invited for these tests.

It was through exposure on local television stations years before that helped in the metamorphosis of Brent Carl, transforming him from a lowly auto body repairman into a multi millionaire safety administrator for the federal government.

Chapter Three

On a bleak and snowy February morning, Brent Carl opened the gates of his compound as he normally did around 6 a.m. under the watchful eye of his security guard. He was startled when another car, a recent model black Lexus with tinted windows, entered through the open gate.

"Excuse me, this is private property." said the security guard.

"Yes, I know." the Lexus driver replied.

"It's alright Blake, sit tight." said Brent, waving off his security.

Brent introduced himself to the stranger in the black Lexus. The two men chatted briefly before Brent instructed the security guard to open the office door.

~~The men then entered the facility from the rear doors, leaving the~~ security guard on the outside.

"So what can I do for you Mr. El Hakim?"

"I have a proposition for you, a way to improve business and earn more money." El Hakim replies.

"Listen, I have all the work the place can handle right now, I can't possibly take on any more testing."

"Not testing." El Hakim said.

Brent went on to explain to the stranger that all of his work came via contract with car companies and requisitions from the federal or state governments. They were not set up to do private testing at this time, due to the sheer quantity of work they already had contracted for.

"That's how it's done here my friend." He said opening the door to the main testing area.

"You crash these cars here and the car companies and the government pays you money to do that, right?" asks El Hakim

"That's it in a nutshell, yes. There are exhaustive reports that are done following the crash tests, reports that go directly to the Department of Transportation and other government agencies, not to mention to the car companies themselves." He said

"How would you like to make ten times the money you are now?"

"Well, who wouldn't, but as I said, I cannot possibly increase the amount of testing we're doing" Carl replied.

"I'm not talking about testing cars; I'm talking about selling cars."

"Selling what, you want to buy the scrap when the tests are completed?"

"No, I want to buy the vehicles before you crash them my friend." El Hakim replied.

"How in the hell do you think we can do that? I mean, the companies send the vehicles to us to do scientific tests on them. They expect 100 page reports on the safety of these vehicles. What exactly are you proposing here?" ask Carl.

"My families have a thirst for this new thing called the SUV, and quite frankly, they can sell as many as they can get their hands on over there."

"Over there?"

"They live Saudi Arabia, in Riyadh to be exact. We can sell these things for one hundred thousand United States Dollars and more. In United States dollars; do you hear me man? We sell them through our connections in the middle east and through websites all over the world."

The more Mr. El Hakim pushed, the more Brent could visualize the millions of dollars in sheer profit.

"How?" Brent replied, obviously becoming hooked.

"It's quite simple Mr. Carl. Your system here becomes sloppy. Your routine begins to misplace the luxury vehicles we want. I know these car companies. By the time they become conscious an error in inventory *may* have been made, the car is being used to take Saudi kids to school."

"I don't believe it can work." A now interested Carl replies.

"But it can sir, and it will. Here is my proposal. You are about to test the new Japanese line of sport utility vehicles, correct?"

"Yes, its common knowledge we're about to begin testing for the Japanese." replied Carl. "It is a very lucrative contract for us, the biggest yet."

El Hakim outlined to Brent how he could successfully orchestrate the disappearance of a single brand new Japanese SUV from the inventory in the hangar beside the testing centre. He furthermore demonstrated how to erase paper trails that follow these vehicles from the manufacturing source.

After weeks of painstaking work on readjusting the actual vehicle records, a Lexus LX470 disappeared from inventory. In fact it never appeared anywhere. The biggest problem for El Hakim and Carl at that time was what to do with this leftover vehicle. Shipping had not been arranged yet, so they were left with the Lexus.

"Got kids that drive?" El Hakim asked of Benson.

"I only have one son, and yes he's old enough to drive." Carl replied.

"In that case, take this Lexus home for him. I'll produce some registration docs and some out of state plates for it. Think he'll like it?" El Hakim asks with a smile.

"Fucking amazing, of course he'll love it." replied Carl.

Subsequent to the success of their practice run, Carl and El Hakim duplicated the scheme and removed from inventory over 200 vehicles of varying description. They were moved away from the Buffalo facility, and then shipped by freighter to the Middle East.

Most popular vehicles on the Middle East requisitions list were the Acura Integra, BMW M Roadster, Cadillac Escalade and GMC Yukon XL, the Audi S4, and Lexus LX, GX or SC model and the Mercury Marauder.

Amazingly, no one, no car company bean counter, no government inspector, no one, had become aware of any discrepancies in the inventory of crash test vehicles.

The Federal Government it seems had been made aware of the

influx of high end vehicles being received in Saudi by a lowly employee of the American Consulate. Car companies were notified of the possible fraud and had offered the government their assistance in launching an investigation.

Not only do car manufacturers affix a serial number in the front dashboard of their vehicles, they also imprint this number in a variety of other locations inside and outside of the vehicle. El Hakim and Carl knew where the car manufacturers had affixed every duplicate serial number and erased them thoroughly.

When the federal government requested the assistance of the Buffalo Police Department, Police Chief Leanne Ronalds appointed A. J. Benson as lead detective. Known for his ability to be politically correct, he was the perfect appointment to work with the feds.

Chapter Four

Several months of surveillance ensued. Benson endured as Brent Carl organized the shipment of new high end vehicles to the Saudi automobile black market. Carl made millions in addition to the colossal amount of money he was being paid by car companies and government agencies to do the actual safety testing. Carl never had to leave the building. He never traveled to the mid east.

The end was near when the car companies agreed to play a part in the sting by affixing high tech satellite based tracking systems to vehicles being sent to Carl for testing. Through this secondary identification system, it was revealed that the missing vehicle identification numbers were from only those vehicles shipped in the previous year or two to the BRIC facility in Buffalo.

Simultaneous raids were made on the black market auto dealer on Airport Road in Riyadh and at the Buffalo testing facility.

Benson and FBI Agent Grant Norman were the first to enter the offices of BRIC.

"Mr. Carl, my name is A. J. Benson; I am with the Buffalo Police Department. This gentleman is FBI agent Grant Norman."

"Nice to meet you gentlemen, what can I do for you" Carl replies.

"You can stand up, put your hands behind your back and listen to your rights."

"What the fuck? Do you know who I am?" barks Carl.

"Brent Carl, you are under arrest. We are charging you with fraud, grand theft and third degree grand larceny, just for starters."

The entire BRIC building had been secured by BPD officers and FBI agents. Several of the agents had accompanied Benson and

Norman inside the testing facility. Only Benson and Norman had entered the office to arrest Brent Carl. They were making their way out of the office and through the test facility toward the rear doors when without warning a loud shot was heard over the heads of all of the officers in the main test area.

"There!" one FBI officer points directly to a metal cat walk above the testing area.

Had all the officers not already had their 45 caliber Glocks out of their holsters, they would not have been able to return the volley of shots that were fired in their direction and effectively exterminate the shooter from above.

Benson and Norman push Carl to the floor, his head hitting the metal encased channel that contains the cable that pull the crash test cars into a concrete barrier.

"Stay down! He orders Carl.

"Grant, you alright?" asks Benson.

There is no reply as FBI agent Grant Norman slumps to the floor of the test centre, his service pistol dropping from his hand and onto the ground. The gun is in clear view of Carl and within reach.

Blood pours from Agent Normans ears and pools underneath his head. A wide gaping hole exposes the fatty tissue of his scalp. Shiny white bone shows through the cavernous hole made by high caliber shell.

"Fuck you!" Carl shrieks as he dives over Norman to retrieve the FBI 45 caliber Browning pistol. He points the Browning directly at A. J. Benson, carelessly aims and squeezes the trigger.

Benson is hit hard on the side of the face and drops to the floor.

Brent Carl was tackled from behind, given a Rodney King-like thumping and finally subdued by four Buffalo Police Department officers. Carl dropped the FBI agent's gun when one officer cracked a night stick over his right forearm, splitting the ulnar bone leaving the arm a swollen broken mess.

FBI and BPD back up units were arriving before the paramedic ambulance. Denied any medical attention at this time, Carl was dragged to a waiting police unit and whisked off.

The arriving paramedic unit was motioned to proceed directly inside the testing facility through the same doors the beautiful upscale SUV's would enter before being crashed into a cement barrier.

After initial treatment to his head wound, the unconscious Benson was lifted into the waiting paramedic ambulance unit. Blood was pouring out of the head wound. The trail left on the test centre floor was substantial and worrisome to the paramedics.

Body removal was summoned.

Following hours of painstaking reconstruction of the event by investigating officers, the bodies of Agent Grant Norman and Mr.Salim El Hakim were removed to the Erie County Medical Examiners Office for autopsy.

Chapter Five

Dr. Stratten seldom speaks with patients in such a forthright and open manner, and certainly not with as much profanity. He loves his older step brother. They have the same mother and different fathers. A. J.'s father died when he was four years old.

Their mother married Mr. Stratten a few years later. Ken Stratten was the only offspring of that union. He always admired his older brother, who even then wanted to be a policeman when he grew up. He never lost sight of that goal and when he was old enough, he applied to the Buffalo New York Police Department.

From his first day of training with the BPD, A. J. was the consummate professional. He lived for work. A. J. was always available for additional training, and extra shift work. Whenever Buffalo would experience a debilitating winter storm, A. J. would rush into work to provide assistance on his day or weekend off.

He would come home from his shift and tell cop stories to the family. He loved the role of policeman right from the first day of training and rookie ride-along shifts.

After a brief but spectacular romance, A. J. married Angela Forgie when he was 22 years old. At 19, she was a tall, very outgoing, red haired beauty. Angela was a transcriptionist with the Buffalo Police. Her job was to transcribe the scribble in police officers notebooks in preparation for court cases.

She became expert at deciphering the scrawling in those little black notebooks that cops clutch in the palm of their hand. A. J. first asked Angela for a date by jotting an invitation in his patrolman's notebook. She uncovered it while transcribing his notes for a trial. They fell in love.

In the beginning their relationship was passionate and hot. They managed to take every opportunity to be with each other, at work and away. They made love at least four times a day, more on weekends and holidays. A.J. and Angela were once discovered by a security officer having sex at the old Buffalo Zoo, huddled under a blanket outside the monkey house. They would take wild weekends away in places like Nassau, New Orleans or Montego Bay. Nine months after the wedding ceremony, A. J. and Angela had a son they named Jimmy.

At about this time Angela became a stay at home mom. She loved her new position in life for a while and didn't seem to miss her career at BPD. After several years of chasing Jimmy around the house, the endless shitty diapers and absentee husband, Angela became restless and on edge.

Angela's increasing habit of patronizing a lineup of local bars frequented by members of the BPD annoyed A. J. He felt if she was out amusing herself, he didn't need to be attentive to her needs. He monitored the situation by regularly soliciting the surveillance help of his cop friends. These friends would report on Angela's activities and who she drank with.

On one dark evening in the middle of a Buffalo winter, Angela crossed the line. As reported by his good friend and fellow BPD officer Dave Alexander, Angela was discovered outside the rear door of the Niagara Tavern. In the unlit parking lot, she waited there with the collar of her coat up over the back of her head. Several regulars of the bar soon joined Angela. One of them was seen with his arm around her, kissing that part of her neck that was still exposed to the howling wind.

The two others entered a large Ford Econoline van, beers in hand. In a short few minutes, Angela and the neck kisser joined the other men in the rear compartment of the van.

Although disturbed by what was unfolding, Alexander continued to maintain surveillance. He wondered if he should intervene, help a friend's wife by getting in the middle of what was going on, or just stay clear and report what he sees. After a brief pause, Officer Alexander moved slowly over to the van and peered into the now nearly fogged windows.

The three men were all over Angela, fondling her naked breasts and fingering between her naked thighs. She moaned and laughed. An obvious willing participant Angela was flipped wildly onto her back, her coat the only protection from the van's dirty floor. Her long legs were elevated and spread wide open. The youngest of the three men was the first to climb on top of Angela and thrust his swollen piece into her manicured nest. Both of the other men maintained a position over Angela, above her head as she alternated their hardness in her mouth.

Angela was enjoying the sexual thrashing she was receiving from these members of the BPD. She constantly sucked on each of their units and received hard poundings by each of the officers.

She was satisfied in every way by two of the men. The other officer, having already succumbed to the excitement of the event, responded by giving Angela a face full of love.

The windows of the van were now too obstructed with condensation to see through. Dave Alexander banged hard on the rear door of the van in an effort to alarm the occupants and hopefully signal the end this event.

From a distance now, he saw the van bounce as the men obviously tugged on their pants and readjusted. All three men soon exited the van, with Angela in tow. They reentered the tavern, where Angela immediately attended to her condition in the ladies room.

Without too much delay, Angela joined the men in a booth in the bar for a few more drinks before leaving the bar to return to her home and her young son.

Other parents from Jimmy's Cub and Boy Scout groups believed Angela was a single parent. Angela took Jimmy to his little league baseball games, swimming lessons and to football practices. A. J. almost never took his son anywhere. He never had that quiet Dad to Son talk unless it was to be critical of something Jimmy had done around the house. He never took his young son to watch airplanes, or trains or a football or hockey game.

A.J. blocked Angela from his day to day life in due course. He replaced her with the need to succeed on the job. He loved the power that being a police officer gave him. Climbing the police department ladder came easy to A. J. He was a well trained cop and played the Police Department politics the right way.

Angela quickly evolved into a love craved, attention seeking manic depressive middle aged woman. A sad contradiction to the youthful beauty she once emblazoned. She dressed in cheap sexy outfits to do the grocery shopping, hoping only to be noticed by other men.

All Angela wanted was some attention, the type of attention she was missing since A.J. had made climbing the ranks of the BPD the only goal in his life. He made no time in his life for her or for their son. In the process, he manufactured himself a solid police career, now holding the position of Detective Inspector.

Chapter Six

Dave Alexander wasted no time in reporting what he saw to A.J. Quiet and subdued at first, Benson took little time to become totally enraged.

"You're full of shit, I don't believe it." he said.

"A.J., it's true, I'm sorry man." responded Alexander.

"Why didn't you stop her from going into the van, before all this happened?"

"A. J., I have the distinct impression that this was not the first time for this. It seemed too organized you know, the way they connected outside the bar." delivered Alexander.

"Were you in on this too, did you fuck her?"

"Hell no man, why are you trying to blame me for this?"

"You had the power to stop this, and you chose not to, you let my wife get fucked by three of my men. That's why Inspector."

"Honest, I don't know who they are, I only know they were in BPD uniforms and were in the bar with everyone else." Dave said.

"Who in the bar knows what happened in the truck?" Benson demanded to know.

Holding back the truth, reserved and visibly shaken, Office Alexander replied "Everyone!"

Chapter Seven

A. J. Benson returned home one evening a few weeks later to find his family home in suburban Amherst completed empty of life. Angela and Jimmy were gone.

Vanished.

The dog too was gone. There was no note, no broken mirrors or glass that might have been the result of some final frustration. Desk drawers and file cabinets that might have contained money or documents were secure and in one piece.

The complete inventory of furniture, television and video equipment, appliances, tables, chairs, beds and dressers was intact. The family was nowhere to be found. Angela's car was in the garage. Jimmy's homework lay on his bedroom desk. The previously frozen pot roast, now thawed, was left on the bottom rack of the fridge.

The discovery of his wife's entire wardrobe only confused A. J. more. Likewise, every article of his son's clothing remained hung in closets or folded in his dresser drawers. Personal items also remained in the home. Angela's make up kit, her toothbrush and hair dye were all left in their place.

"What the fuck is that?" A. J. had said out loud as he searched the house for clues.

Something had alarmed him, some sound, something audible but muffled in the house. He could hear the sound coming from the study.

A closer examination of the study revealed a desktop telephone off the hook. Picking it up and listening into receiver A.J. heard someone speaking.

"Cloudy and high of 7 or 44 degrees." he heard the recording.

"Current time is 4:45 p.m. and you should expect overnight frost with freezing temperatures in the Highlands and Eastern Coast." the tape continued

Chapter Eight

Buffalo is one of those Northeastern U. S. cities that receive a lot of negative attention in movies, television and by stand up comics.

You know you're from Buffalo if:

**You design your kids Halloween costume to fit over a snowsuit,*

**Driving is better in winter because the pot holes are filled with snow,*

**You think sexy lingerie is tube socks and flannel pajamas,*

**You know that even with the lightest threat of snow, Buffalo schools will be closed,*

**You realize there is nothing "International" about Buffalo International Airport.*

In actual fact quite a beautiful city, Buffalo receives branding as a lunch pail city due to its past prominence as an industrial hub specializing in steel and chemical production, not to mention the wicked snow storms during winter months. The Queen city is nestled along the south shore of Lake Erie at the mouth of the mighty Niagara River.

Buffalo is a very cosmopolitan city with a generous mixing of old and new architecture. Theatres and other venues for the arts attract visitors to Buffalo from both sides of the international border. Buffalo is multicultural and thriving. There are several universities and colleges in Buffalo making it a hip city to live in. It has professional hockey, football and baseball teams. Most of the abandoned heavy industrial areas of the past have been reborn into lakeside townhouse complexes and beautiful parks. Marinas with every description pepper the lakefront and the Niagara River waterway.

Travel across the Peace Bridge and you arrive in the town of Fort Erie, in the province of Ontario Canada. It is somewhat a dreary town, some visitors even referring to it as Dreary Fort Erie.

Fort Erie was significant as a British stronghold during the war against the United States in 1812. The fort still remains there as a tourist attraction. It was near the old fort, in the mid 1980's the bodies of 29 American Militia were discovered buried by a local resident digging the foundation for his new home.

Killed during heavy battles in and around the Fort, the soldiers were buried expeditiously without dignity. Some were dumped unceremoniously into mass graves from ox driven carts during the nighttime battle. One grave with bodies even contained remains of the ox and wagon.

A. J. had been part of a contingency of Buffalo police personnel dispatched to assist Canadian and American authorities at the original body excavation site. He assisted members of the Mortuary Division of the American Army as they lifted the skeletal remains from the makeshift cemetery. A casket company from Indiana was contracted by the American Army to provide the 29 solid steel caskets to hold the remains of the fallen servicemen that died in a battle in a war long forgotten by most.

Working with the archaeologists and medical personnel down in the grave caused A. J. to be moved emotionally by the experience. He talked about this event incessantly to anyone who would listen.

He is captivated by the condition of the bodies and how they were found after being buried for 170 years. He discussed with archaeologists about how time, temperature and soil conditions act on decomposing the human body.

He began to fixate on this encounter in very macabre ways. He spent hours reflecting about how a body would decompose in the ground and how these bodies would have gone unnoticed for all these years.

A. J. and other police personnel have seen the horror of death as a regular part of their job. They are used to viewing the results of disasters, small and large. They see the truly unpleasant. They have smelled rotten or burnt flesh. They have touched and handled the dead at various stages of decomposition. From a body freshly deceased or the bodies retrieved from the Niagara River after three months underwater A. J. has been involved in some horrific cases. He has seen the cruel underbelly of society.

His experience at Fort Erie was different.

This was the first time A. J. had ever seen the actual skeletal remains of a human being. He was amazed at how wide of the mark his perception was about the color of the human bones, that they were browner in color than the usual stark white color we associate skeletons to be. He learned how soil conditions and length of time buried effect the color of human bone.

A. J. Benson became an armchair expert on skeletons. He got to know all of the joints and bones of the human skeleton; he could tell you how to differentiate male and female skeletal remains. He could name most of the 300 or so bones that make up a human skeleton.

An international funeral service was conducted at The Old Fort Erie with the flag draped caskets of the 1812 American service men resting with honor in the main staging area of the Fort. Afterward, an impressive procession of 30 hearses from both sides of the border drove to Bath New York for ceremonies to finally bury the veterans in U. S. soil. In true U. S. Army preparation, they had 30 hearses in the procession but had only 29 caskets. This was done in the event that one of the hearses had a breakdown or flat tire enroute to the cemetery. The preparations paid off because one of the hearses did experience an overheating problem on the Interstate.

This unique funeral remains as the only time in history that American soldiers were repatriated from Canada.

His friendship with a local funeral director Harry Ridgeway provided the opportunity for A. J. to ride in one of the hearses provided by Buffalo funeral homes in the procession to the military cemetery in Bath, NY.

Historically significant, Buffalo is also where the 24th American

President, William McKinley was assassinated on September 6, 1901. The President was eliminated while attending the Pan-American Exposition there. He had just spent the afternoon sightseeing at Niagara Falls with his wife.

Another famous American with Buffalo roots was Millard Fillmore, a lawyer who practiced law in Buffalo before he was elected President of the United States in 1850. He died in Buffalo in 1874.

Chapter Nine

The drive from the downtown Buffalo medical centre to the home of his step brother takes Dr. Stratten north of the City into the suburbs and to the town of Amherst. Amherst has the distinction of being one of the safest cities in America to live. Travel is easy in this area. Ample multi lane expressways that bounder the suburbs take most of the commercial traffic away from the small communities north of Buffalo making the evening drive for the doctor unhurried and somewhat carefree.

The two storey Bricks home on Coronation Drive is easy to find, just off the Millersport Highway, then north on meandering Sweet Home Road. Dr. Stratten is impressed with the outside appearance of the home and how A. J. has kept this home so nice since the disappearance of Angela and Jimmy.

He had not visited his brother's home since the death of their mother a few years ago.

Dr. Stratten recalls all the good times in that home as he rings the doorbell. Trying to inject some humor into the situation, he leans into the oak door and says in a loud voice "OK, the doctors making a house call, open up chicken shit."

There is no reply from inside.

"Come on A. J., I see your car here, I know you're home." He shouts.

Surprised to find the door unlocked, Dr. Stratten enters the neat house expecting to catch his brother mid pee or perhaps in the shower. The house décor and contents are no different than the last time he was there for a family get together.

"A.J!" he called, but still no reply.

The note was on the kitchen table beside several empty cans of Genesee Cream Ale.

My Dear Doctor Brother:

You're right, I am a mess. I feel sick most of the time and know that leaving now is the best remedy for my sick life. BPD has granted my request for time off. You're right, they will survive without me. So off I go. By the time you read this I will have begun my search. I should have started searching years ago.

Love to all,

A. J.

The most direct route to Europe from Buffalo is making the 90 minute drive to Pearson International Airport in Toronto Canada. Buffalo has an excellent airport but all of the European international flights connect in New York City, Chicago or Washington. So in an effort to conserve time and money, A. J. has chosen the Canadian route.

He waits not so patiently in the brand new terminal at Toronto for his evening flight. He wonders the concourses amongst the holiday travelers. Sensing he was developing a little objectionable body odor, he visited the perfume duty free store to spray on a few samples. The charming young woman who waited on A. J. asked him all kinds of customer service questions. "Do you like fruity or flowery, strong or light scents" she would ask. All he wanted was a shot of something on his clothes to hide the smell of booze and smoke.

"I should have done this a long time ago." he said to a woman sitting beside him.

"Done what?" she responds.

"Start searching for someone, that's all."

"Is this person missing?"

"I guess you could call it that. They both are."

It seems to A. J. that he has been sitting in the waiting area at gate B3 for a long time. The beer buzz fading, he knew he didn't have time for more alcohol. He had made a brief stop at the duty free outlet before crossing over the Peace Bridge into Canada, enroute to Toronto and subsequently consumed all the booze while driving. His rental car is littered with empty beer cans from that excursion.

"Finally!" he said to the woman, as he listens to the boarding announcement for British Airways Flight #92, nonstop Boeing 777 service to London Heathrow.

Chapter Ten

Hogmanay is the name Scots give to New Years Eve, a celebration they have made all their own with a unique mix of tradition, hedonism, sentimentality and enthusiasm. The roots of Hogmanay are in ancient pagan festivities based around the winter solstice, which in most places gradually merged with Christmas.

When hard line Scottish Protestant clerics in the sixteenth century abolished Christmas for being a Catholic Mass, the Scots, not wanting to miss out on a mid-winter knees-up, instead put their energy into greeting the New Year.

Houses were cleaned from top to bottom, debts were paid and quarrels made up, and after the bells of midnight were run, great emphasis was put on welcoming good luck into your house. This still takes the form of the tradition "first footing" or visiting your neighbors bearing gifts.

The ideal first guest of the New Year was a tall, dark haired male carrying a bottle of whisky. Women or redheads on the other hand, were bad luck, though no one carrying a bottle of whisky seemed to be turned away.

All this neighborly greeting meant that a fair bit of partying went on, and of course, no one is expected to go to work the next day.

A. J. pays his three pound thirty at the inside ticket booth and is given directions to the platform while still buzzing from beer served on his connecting flight from London. Helping enhance the euphoria is the pints he managed to guzzle upon arrival in hospitable Edinburgh Airport Pub. He already has a pocket full of heavy coins, his change from paying for his pints with pound notes because he can't figure out the value of each coin.

He notices the Airlink Shuttle approach with its destination sign reading "*Waverley.*" With no time for another pint of Tennants at the terminal pub, he boards the bus, single bag in hand and heads for the top deck of the double decked coach for the 10 mile journey to Edinburgh City Centre.

With Hogmanay approaching, it seemed the whole world was headed to Edinburgh to enjoy the big name bands in the massive city centre street party on New Years Eve. At midnight, a huge fireworks display will be set off over Edinburgh Castle and from the hills surrounding the City.

The Edinburgh Hogmanay is one of the most spectacular New Years celebrations in the entire world.

Along the approach to the city centre A. J. catches his first glimpse of Edinburgh Castle, set high above the city. Beneath the castle, the Princess Street Gardens is filled with people strolling and enjoying the amusement rides erected for the celebrations. A huge Ferris wheel dwarfs the monument in memory of Walter Scott in the park that lines Princess Street. He observes people skating on an outdoor rink in the lower level of the park near a museum. The City bustles with activity during these rainy few days before Hogmanay. Christmas decorations adorn the buildings in the commercial district opposite the park. A. J. is immediately impressed with the City of Edinburgh and hopes that it will be an easy place for him to navigate while conducting his search.

He makes a mental note to return to Jenners Department Store as he passes the huge multi storied building. His hair still wet from the constant rain is a reminder he needs an umbrella. The coach glides into the City Centre, turns onto the wide street and comes to an abrupt stop.

The driver announces "Waverley Station! This is the last stop."

Bag in hand, A. J. climbs down from his vantage point in the coach and spills out onto the street in front of Waverley Station.

A steep sloped walkway leads him down into the main concourse of the railway terminal where he immediately spots Chester's, the terminal pub. Oblivious to the hundreds of scurrying passengers, non stop departure announcements and the idling engines of a parade of sleek black taxicabs, A. J. follows a direct path directly to his next drink.

Dropping his worn bag onto the tile floor, he occupies a bar stool at the end of the bar.

"Tennants." he replies to the barmaid's enquiry.

"Cheers." she says as the pint of frothy fluid is lowered onto a dirty coaster.

Travel has a way of affecting an individual in many ways. When most people arrive at their destination, they experience a type of euphoria, a peaceful feeling, of having accomplished what was set out to do. A. J. felt no euphoria whatsoever. Other than the steady intake of alcohol, he had not accomplished very much at all.

Perched on the bar stool in Chester's terminal pub at Waverley Station in Edinburgh he resembled all the other weary travelers who craved a pint or two before or after their journey.

A. J. had the feeling he should be moving forward in his search efforts. The overly friendly barmaid in Chester's helped him forget his mission.

Erin wasted no time telling A. J. that she was originally from a small town in the Highlands, and had recently moved to Edinburgh to work and attend university. She loved footy. Her favorite team is the Hearts. She lived alone not far from the train station. She had no sisters or brothers. Her father died two years ago. Her mother lives in France. She does not have a boyfriend. She is 22. Her life is condensed into working in a terminal pub and flirting with strangers.

The steady intake of Tennants helps A. J. realize he is about to fall in love. Erin has the same feelings, fueled not by alcohol but by the charming well dressed and seemingly flamboyant cop from the states who is actually leaving a tip for her after every beer he orders. Tipping is not the norm in Britain like it is in the United States.

"You'll be here for a while, ya?" Erin bluntly asks.

"Not sure hun." A.J. replies

"What time does your train leave?" she enquires.

"No train sweetie, I just arrived here on the coach from the airport. This is the last stop on the route, I had to get off here." quips A. J.

"So we should have a meal?"

"I suppose I should eat today." A. J. replies.

"What do you like?" she asks.

"I don't want any of that haggis shit you people eat over here." he grunts.

"I don't like it either. Its tourist food, but most pubs have it on their menu. How about some bangers and mash, I know a great place?" she said.

"What the fuck is bangers and mash?" he asks.

"I'm off in ten minutes, I'll take you to a place and show you what bangers and mash is, how's that?

"Another pint Erin." he orders. "Let me try one of these Caledonian things." he orders, pointing at the little sign on the beer tap.

"Cheers." as the 80 schilling higher alcohol beer is placed onto the same dirty coaster.

The cab ride to the restaurant took only ten minutes just over the George IV Bridge from Waverley Station. Monster Mash Cafe is on Forest Road, not far from the University of Edinburgh and the Museum of Scotland. Featuring Edinburgh's famous Crombies sausages and the best mash potatoes in Scotland the cafe is a small rather austere looking place with about 10 tables. Chicken and beef pies and huge pieces of battered fish and tasty chips complement the menu. It's a simple place, offering a respite for those looking to slip away and have a good meal and quiet conversation.

The cooks and servers are from all over the world, working on visas or just trying to make some money to travel. The staff is known for their friendly cheerful service.

Erin and A. J. are greeted by the manager of Monster Mash, a well spoken Irish implant by the name of Liam. He has flaming red hair and blue running shoes.

Liam puts them totally at ease as they choose a seat in the rear of the café. They settle in for A.J.'s first meal since the flight from Toronto to London.

A. J. and Erin spare no time in ordering beer from their waitress Allison, who sits down with them at the table to take their order. Allison is a Canadian, working and taking some Uni courses. Days off are spent working on her yoga and seeing the great country of Scotland. Erin encourages A. J. to order the sausages made with Guinness Stout, a strong black heavy beer. She orders the same, with mash potatoes and leek soup.

"Great! Sausages with beer in them, perfect, I love it here already." said A. J.

"You can't get reekin on the sausages though. You'll need to drink the beer for that." says Erin, as she turns to order two more bottles of Caledonian.

"So big man, what's your story?" She asks of A.J. "You told me you're on a mission of sorts. What mission?"

"I've come to bring my wife and son home to the States with me." he blurts, the beer obviously working like truth serum.

"Your what and who?" Erin reacts.

"My wife and son left me. Disappeared more like, a few years ago. We had some trouble in the relationship. No, we had a lot of trouble and it was mainly because I was so fucking focused on my job. You see Erin, I'm a policeman, a detective in Buffalo. It's western New York state."

"Are you on the job here in Scotland, is that what you mean?" Erin asks.

"No, I'm actually on sick leave right now. It's a long story. I'll fill you in on that later OK? When my wife and son went missing, along with the family dog I might add, I listened to a recording I received on our phone. It was as if someone had dialed the time and temperature number, then left the phone off the hook."

He continued "I listened to it over and over, and determined that the message was from here, in Scotland. It said something like the weather in the Highlands and gave the temperature in both Fahrenheit and centigrade. Angela's family is from this area in Scotland." He matter of factly reports.

"They came to the U.S. from Falkirk in the early 30's and settled in Buffalo. I ignored the obvious for a long time, thinking that living alone was better for me and I reasoned that if Angela had taken Jimmy with her to Scotland, which was ok with me because they would be with her grandparents who I believe still live in Falkirk. I believed seriously that I could be more productive on the job, more focused on work than on a cheating wife and needy kid."

"Cheating?" asks Erin.

"I guess it was my fault for this too, but Angela started hanging around a cop bar in Buffalo, got drinking and smoking dope and fucking everything in sight she could."

"Who looked after your son?"

"She did during the day, then babysitters at night when I wasn't home." A. J. replied. She was quite the girl, embarrassed the hell out of me on one grand night of hers. I found out about it almost as quick as it happened. I had another cop who is also my best friend, follow her into a gang bang of sorts."

"After 4 or 5 guys fucked her in the back of a van, she went right back into the bar to drink some more before bringing her sloppy ass back home."

"Oh my God A. J., how did you cope?" asks Erin.

"Guess I didn't Erin. Not really. Cops are taught to bury their emotions, look the other way, swallow hard and turn away from the bad things that happen. I guess that's what I did. I buried it all. It's hard to bury your feelings and emotions. To sweep all the shit about Angela under the carpet seemed like a reasonable thing to do for me, at least for a while."

"How long can things stay buried?" asked Erin.

"Bodies can stay buried for a long long time Erin, but emotions and feelings come to the surface much faster. That's what I'm dealing with now."

Chapter Eleven

The food and the beer flowed for a couple of hours while Erin and A. J. shared their stories and got reekin, the Scottish slang for being completely drunk. Erin had explained how she fell out with her parents over a man and moved from the Highlands into Edinburgh to get away. She hadn't seen her parents in years. Her parents split, and then divorced just before her father died. Her mother had moved to France with a new boyfriend while Erin began her life as a barmaid at Chesters.

"So where do you think they are A. J.?" asks Erin.

"Not sure really, but I am going to start in Falkirk."

"It's not far from here you know, we can go whenever you want." Erin offers.

"What do you mean? We? You don't need to be involved in this and I don't need help." snaps A. J.

"You're not from here, you don't know the geography and you can't understand some of the people when they speak to you. I can help. Fuck, you didn't even know what a banger is. I want to help."

"Why do you want to help me, we just met?"

"You seem very troubled and disturbed. Besides that, I like you. You seem cool. I can tell that you are uneasy about this search of yours. Please A. J., let me help?" she begs.

"Let's get out of here." he quips as he signals Allison to bring the bill for dinner.

"It's pretty inexpensive eh, only forty five quid for all that food and beer?" Erin says.

"Where are we off to now Erin?"

"It's early still. Let me stop at Chesters on the way and I'll let them know I won't be in for a couple of days."

"On the way where for shit sake?"

"Falkirk! The train leaves every hour this time of day. We'll get there in an hour and rest up. Tomorrow we start the search for your family."

"Are all you Scottish Lassies so goddamn pigheaded and pushy?" he quips.

"Aye, we are my friend, get used to it." Erin replies.

Chapter Twelve

The Falkirk area occupies a central position in Scotland, on the key north-south and east-west motorway and rail routes and within easy reach of Edinburgh and Glasgow airports. No part of Scotland has a better situation both for access from England and for access to other parts of Scotland. It has become renowned as the location for Scotland's first structural icon on the 21st century, The Falkirk Wheel.

The Wheel was opened by Queen Elizabeth II in May of 2002. Nothing like it has ever been built before anywhere in the world. Boat lifts are nothing new. But a rotating boat lift is. The Falkirk Wheel is the largest piece of functional structure in the world. Boats approaching from the higher Union Canal now connect with The Forth and Clyde Canal, an old relic canal of past first opened in 1790.

Boats progress through a 168meter long tunnel that emerges at the start of a 104 meter concrete aqueduct. The far end of this aqueduct opens directly into the upper of the two "gondolas" of the Falkirk Wheel.

The Wheel then rotates and having descended, what is now the lower gondola opens out into a 100 meter circular basis whose landscaping carefully conceals its origins as an open cast pit.

One side of this is a beautiful curved structure of the visitors centre. One final lock at the far end of the basin lowers boats to the level of the Forth and Clyde Canal.

The Falkirk Wheel is a major tourist attraction for the area. It is 35 meters or 115 feet high, the height of eight double decked buses. Each gondola contains 300 tonnes of water, meaning that the Wheel moves 600 tonnes of water on each lift. But because the gondolas are always in balance, because boats displace their own weight of water, moving them takes surprisingly little power. Up to eight boats can be carried at any one time.

The train trip from Waverley Station to Falkirk High Station takes about 50 minutes on the high speed line. There are two railway stations in Falkirk. The High Station and the other, near the centre of town called Grahamston Station.

A. J. and Erin ponder the events of the past few hours after they leave the train. Standing on the platform, the two loners look at each other and embrace.

A. J. dropped his miserable excuse for a suitcase onto the platform and provides a welcome return to the embrace initiated by Erin. A. J. lifts his head slightly to kiss Erin directly hard on her open mouth. They maintain the kiss for a minute until a train, heading in the opposite direction startles them.

"Where to A. J.?" Erin asks.

"I need a drink for sure, how bout you Erin?"

"I'm with you on that, I know a place here. Let's get a cab, it's too far to walk."

Erin and A. J. descend the stairs from the elevated platform into the parking lot of the station. There, several plain cabs wait. A. J. notices the big difference here from the line up of sleek black cabs lined up at Waverley.

They approach the first cab and enter the rear seat. Erin directs the driver to an address in the center of the Town of Falkirk.

The Battle of Falkirk was fought there on July 22, 1298, and saw the defeat of William Wallace by King Edward I and saw the occupation of Scotland by the British until Robert the Bruce's victory at the Battle of Bannockburn in 1314.

It was the first battle in which the longbow proved decisive. Many landmarks in the area bear the Wallace name, including Wallace Street in central Falkirk, the home of the grandparents of Angela Forgie.

The cab ride took only 5 minutes from Falkirk High Station to the

Station Pub. Erin had stayed in this pub on another occasion when she visited Falkirk. The rooms are small with limited furnishings but clean and well maintained. The most attractive benefit to A. J. and Erin is the pub located on the street level just below their room.

The Station Pub is directly across the street from the other Falkirk railway station, Grahamston. It is a typical Scottish pub with two billiard tables, a couple of coin operated gambling machines, televisions tuned to football and a comfortable bar.

Banners of The Falkirk Football Clubs hang behind the bar. The pub is a local hangout, not frequented much by out of towners except railway passenger's crossing over the street for a pint while waiting for a train.

"Two Caledonian Hun!" orders A. J. to the young barmaid.

She obliges by pulling two magnificent pints of the strong beer and then delivering them to the table A. J. and Erin have occupied across the room.

"Cheers." she says as she places the pints on the table.

"Oh, ya cheers, ya, ok" A. J. stumbles to answer.

"We always say cheers when anyone gives us anything at all A. J. Just go with the flow man. If any Scotsman says Cheers, just say Cheers back to him." Erin instructs.

"A. J., tell me where we're going now, how do we find your family?"

"This is only a guess at best Erin, but Angela's grandparents lived in Falkirk. Her parents came to the United States but the old folks wanted to stay put. As far as her grandparents were concerned, their streets were paved with enough gold, and they didn't need to go to the States in order to find prosperity and happiness. Not so for her parents, so they loaded up and set out for the states. They found their way to Buffalo New York. That's where the work was in those days. Her father got a job in the factory at Hooker Chemical. It was stinking work and unhealthy, but it paid the bills. They had a son Brandon and daughter, who was my wife Angela."

"So we're going to the grandparents home are we lad?" Erin asks.

"Yes, I'd like to start there tomorrow. I believe that Angela left the telephone off the hook after calling someone in Scotland. Somehow during the disconnect, the phone went over to the time and temperature recording for this area."

"I believe that she wanted me to follow her here to Scotland. I never did. Not till now. I hope her grandparents can tell me where she is. She and Jimmy may be living with them. I don't love her any more, but I want to know where she is. There was a time when we were extremely close, and it was the best time of my life. We always held hands in public, showed our loved openly for each other. We were inseparable in those days. I didn't want kids, but Angela did, so we compromised. I told her I would go along with having a child as long as she agreed to stay home with the kid. She agreed. Angela worked on the police department too. She knew how demanding the life of a police officer was and is. She knew I wanted to make something of myself on the force, make a name for myself, and be respected by my peers and superiors. But that's tomorrow's business."

Erin, in a quiet whispering voice says "I am very tired and extremely pissed. Will you take me upstairs to bed now?"

She kisses A. J.'s ear and licks his earlobe as she places her hand on his now bulging pants. He returns the affection with a deep open mouth kiss as his chair skids closer to her.

From the other side of the room a table of footballers yell out to the couple "Get a room!"

They did.

Chapter Thirteen

Morning came early for A.J. and Erin as they awoke to the sounds of railway engines from the Great North Eastern Railway reverberate through Grahamston Station. Erin lay naked under a thick woolen blanket as A.J. rolled to one side and slung his legs over the bed. In a sitting position he felt the banging of his brain against his skull, the result of over enjoying strong Scottish beer. Most people in Great Britain consider American beer weak and flavorless compared to Scottish brew.

A.J. manages to stand, moves one foot carefully in front of the other to maneuver to the water closet. He drops down onto the toilet seat with a bang that startles Erin.

"Are ye alright Luv?" she calls out.

There is no immediate reply, only a moaning of sorts from the small washroom built into the corner of the room.

"Erin, wake up, you have to leave now." orders Benson.

"What are ye beakin about?" she replies.

"I've thought about this, I don't need your help, you'll only be in the way here. Thank you, but this is my business, my assignment" he states as he drops face first into the bed."

"A.J. we talked about this last night, don't you remember?"

"I don't remember too much about last night." he replies.

"Do you remember kissing me at the train station?" she asks.

"Of course" he replies "It was nice."

"Do you remember having dinner at Monster Mash in Edinburgh?" she asks.

"Yes, beer in the food, what could be better?"

"Do you remember fucking me for hours when we came upstairs from the pub last night?" her questions becoming quicker and reflective of how boiling hot mad she was getting.

"Yes, I do remember, but searching for my family is where I draw the line. This is my responsibility, my doings and……."

A. J. was cut off mid sentence when Erin rolled onto him as he lay on his back. Looking at him eyebrow to eyebrow and nose to nose from on top of him she said

"Then you remember that I *am* helping you find your family."

"Yes, I know we talked about that. I didn't plan on anyone helping me once I got here. Meeting you was wonderful and you are wonderful, but you cannot get involved in my search. Thank you for the lovely afternoon and evening, and for the company at dinner last night, but please Erin, just go back to your flat in Edinburgh. Go back to work at Chester's, forget me, please." He pleads.

'Flamin hell A. J., what was this all about, you fed me just enough bullshit to give me a thrashing last night, is that all this is?"

"Of course not. You are a great person." he replied calmly.

With her finger pointed directly at A. J.'s face, a very vocal Erin says "So you've told me three or four times now! Who else is here to help you? I know we just met, but we have something, we have each other here and no one else, so please let me help you?"

A. J. takes Erin's hands and places them at her side, then takes her undecorated face in his hands and says "Go home. Go back to work Erin. I'll see you at Chester's in a few days. They'll need you to work with Hogmanay in a few days. I promise to come to you, but Erin, I need to do this by myself."

"Bloody hell!" she rants "Bloody hell."

Dejected and feeling like a well used overnight whore, Erin adjusts the water temperature and slips into the small shower stall. Water running over her head and face cover the tears she is crying but her sobbing is heard by A. J. outside the bathroom. His head hangs low as he rubs his still aching forehead. He moves to the bed where his clothes from the night before have been slung and dresses quickly. In an attempt to avoid the still sobbing barmaid, A. J. picks his bag up and takes his leave.

He listens for a minute or two outside the door and hears the shower still running, but the sobbing has stopped. He retreats down the hallway to the stairs that lead into the pub. A brief stop to ask directions, and he is gone. The search for Angela has really begun.

Wallace Street appears to A. J. to be a short walk from the Station Pub. Bag in hand he makes his way down the cobblestone sidewalks of this quaint village. He cannot help to reflect on Angela, her parents and grandparents, and how it must have been years ago to live in Falkirk, when motor cars were as scarce as the food supply for your family. The work in those days must have been hard. Angela's grandfather had been a journeyman carpenter. He would travel wherever the work was. He spent a lot of time on the road, leaving his wife alone to raise the family a great deal of the time.

When his son and wife expressed an interest in moving to North America, Angela's father thought his parents would jump at the chance to start a new life. They were shocked and surprised that the feelings of the old couple were not the same as the next generation. They felt things were fine in Falkirk. Hard, but hardships build character and gave meaning to life.

The elder couple supported their son's desire to move to North America. They had no idea where Buffalo was. Niagara Falls meant nothing to them. They were small town Scottish folk and wanted to stay that way. So, on a warm spring day, the family gathered at 67 Wallace Street to bid farewell to Angela's parents. After several toasts with the local malt, the young couple walked the kilometer to Grahamston Station with their belongings. The train ride terminated in Glasgow, where the couple made their way to the Ocean Terminal to meet the boat that would take them to New York City.

They arrived in New York a week later. Before taking the Erie Lackawanna Railway train to Buffalo, they toured as much of the great city of New York as they could look anxiously for the streets that were paved with gold. The train for Buffalo left from New York that evening for the overnight trip to Buffalo. The overnight trip to new life, a new house full of happy children and a promising new job with a large chemical manufacturer.

Approaching Wallace Street, A. J. noticed the now familiar yellow and red sign advertising Tennants Lager in the corner window of a quaint local pub. Not being able to resist, he entered the small pub, ordered his pint of Tennants. He gulped his breakfast pint so fast the barman had not even had a chance to return A. J.'s change.

"Keep it, but bring me another pint." He orders.

The pint is placed in front of A.J. who is now comfortably perched on a bar stool directly in the middle of the bar and in front of the beer taps.

"Cheers all." He exclaims to all who could hear him.

The only other person in the bar that early in the morning was the barman.

"Cheers mate. Where you from?"

"The States." A. J. replies.

The brief pause coupled with the look on the barman's face told A. J. that Americans may not be too popular for some reason.

"Being from the States ok around here is it?" A. J. asks.

"Be better if you said you were Canadian." A patron responds.

"Why?" A. J. enquires.

"No reason mate, guess we're all still pretty pissed at how your buddy Bush suckered our Prime Minister into the Iraq war." replied the barman. "Why can't you lot stay out of every else's fight? The Canadian Prime Minister told Bushy that it was none of their business, pound salt up your ass he said; we're not fighting a war a world away. Gotta give the Canucks big points for that one eh?"

"Bullshit! Another Tennants." an angry A. J. orders.

"Cheers man. So what you doing in Falkirk, seeing the wheel?" asks the barman.

"No wheel. I'm looking for someone. They might be living with an older couple right here on Wallace Street. Woman's name is Angela. Her grandparents live up there at number sixty nine. Know them?"

"Them?" Laddy, old man Forgie has been dead for a long time now. Just the old lady living there now. Christ man, she must be near 90 years old." States the barman matter of factly.

"Have you ever seen that woman around, Angela I told you her name was, ever see her, or see a little boy with her?" asks Benson.

"No, can't say that I have. Let me think on that one a minute."

The barman contemplates these questions carefully and before replying to A. J. picks up the phone on the bar and dials a number.

"Hun, have a bloke here, American fellow, looking for one of the Forgie's. Is there been anyone staying with the wee old woman lately?" the barman requests.

"Not seen her lately, how long? Any kid with her, little boy? Aye, aye, aye" as the barman receives information in his earpiece. 'Cheers hun, I'll be home for my tea, regular time."

"Well lad, you may be in luck. Seems that the old lady had someone staying with her a while back. The wife's not sure how long though. Said she was a pretty girl, but no mention of a kid though."

"What did she look like?" asks A. J.

"Want me to ring the wife back?"

"No, fuck no, that's good enough, I'll go and check the place out on my own." Benson replies.

"Girl hasn't been here for a while, so the wife says."

"Thanks for your trouble old timer. Cheers."

A. J. finished his final breakfast pint and headed directly to the side door and out on to Wallace Street.

Walking quickly now, he discovers the odd numbered houses are on the left side of the street, so he crosses over and notes the numbers on the front of the modest row of dwellings.

A. J. estimates these homes were probably built around the turn of the century. The homes were small; multi storied little places, each with a separate entrance. At number sixty-nine, a small well kept yard graces the front of the little home. Benson notes the pleasant flower patterned window coverings. The place looks neat and well kept and he wonders if the old lady has had some help recently keeping the place up. Is it Angela that helps around the little place to make it look so appealing from the street?

"Is she in there? A. J. asks himself audibly.

The big brave cop from the States pensively paces in front of the home for several minutes. Not wanting to draw too much attention to himself, he proceeds over to the door at number sixty-nine and pushes the little white button that rings a buzzer just inside the door.

Looking through a crack in the window covering the door, A. J. sees no sign of anyone on the inside of the house. He cups his hands over his eyes to get a better look but is not rewarded.

Is the place empty, or has my brother called over here to tell them I have come to get my family?" A. J. thinks out loud.

As soon as A. J. turned his back and glanced up the street, the front door of number sixty nine opens quickly, catching the chain lock in the process. The sound of the chain hitting the hardwood door makes a loud cracking noise that frightens A. J., who was miles away in thought.

"Canna help you?" a little voice asks through the small opening in the door.

"Are you Mrs. Forgie?" A. J. asks.

"Aye."

"Mrs. Forgie, I am your granddaughters husband A. J., from Buffalo New York, can I come in please?" asks Benson.

"I don't remember having a granddaughter sir, I think you are mistaken. Good bye." She says as she closes the door on Benson.

Benson is awe struck, his mouth hanging up as if to be waiting for someone to feed him.

"What the fuck?" he says as he knocks on the door hard to attract the old ladies attention again.

"What is it ye want son? I am alone here."

"Mrs. Forgie, please let me in, I am a police officer", A. J. says as if requesting permission to search a house.

The old lady again peeked through the door after opening it up to the bang of the chain. She removes the chain and allows A. J., the policeman, to enter.

"Mrs. Forgie, I am your granddaughter Angela's husband. Do you remember your granddaughter? Do you remember your son and his wife, who moved to the States?"

"Yes, I think I do." the frail old lady replies.

"Has Angela been living here with you for a while now?"

"Oh yes, I remember her. She's not here any more." The woman replies.

"Where is she now, Angela, where is she?"

"I dunno son, she's gone from this place."

"The boy, where is the boy?" A. J. demands.

"No boy here, just the girl and I, but she's gone now.'

Frustrated at not getting the answers he wants, A. J. became impatient with the old woman, who by now he believes is suffering from Alzheimer's disease or dementia of some sort.

"Listen old girl, where is Angela? You know Angela don't you? Your granddaughter, and her son Jimmy, where are they?" he demands.

"Oh, the boy, he's dead." Says the old woman.

"Dead? Dead? What do you mean dead?"

"Drown. In the river, fishing with his father. Father couldn't save him. Terrible thing." The woman explains.

"But I'm Jimmy's father. Don't you realize that? Where is Angela? Where are they both?"

The sound of a motor interrupts the questioning of the old woman. A small blue Vauxhall pulls up along side number sixty seven and empties its passengers out onto the sidewalk.

"Hi Grammie" a voice says as she enters the house.

A. J. freezes in his place. How lucky could he be to find his wife this soon after arriving in Falkirk? Frozen he anticipates what his next words should be. How does he explain his uncaring actions, not looking for her and Jimmy sooner. How does he talk to her about his son? Is he dead? Dread and shock enter his body. He is no longer angry at being abandoned. He is thankful that after all this time she appears to him.

The woman enters the small dwelling and glances up at Benson. The short, stocky woman with white hair is puzzled at why this man is standing in her grandmother's home.

"Good Morning Miss." says A. J. disappointed that the woman is not his wife.

"Good Morning to you sir, who might you be?"

"My name is A. J. Benson, I am married to Angela Forgie, and I'm looking for her."

"Why would she be here, we know of no one by that name here, do we Gram?" the woman replies

"So who are you?" A. J. asks puzzled.

"My name is Gloria, I'm Mildred's daughter."

"This is your mother?" A. J. asks as he points to the old lady.

"Yes, this is my mother Mildred Mink." Gloria says.

"I am looking for Mrs. Forgie, who lives at number sixty nine Wallace Street."

"Oh my god, Mrs. Forgie has not lived here for a couple of years. My grammie came to live with Mrs. Forgie when my father passed on. Then Mrs. Forgie passed on and left the house to my Grammie."

"What's this all about Mr. Benson?"

"My wife is Angela Forgie, granddaughter of Mrs. Forgie. We had some problems in our marriage and she left me and took our son with her. No notice, no advanced warning, she just left me high and dry. She didn't take any money, clothes or any of my son's belongings. His homework from school was still on his desk. I should have started looking for her a long time ago, but for a lot of selfish reasons, I didn't. Until now. Do you know her?"

"There was never anyone who visited with Mrs. Forgie. I never saw her son and daughter, although they called on holidays, and certainly the granddaughter and great grandson never visited her here." Gloria replies.

A. J. is completely taken aback by this news. He thought for certain, that Angela was going to be here with Jimmy. But, the old lady Forgie is also dead.

"Well then Gloria, who is the kid your mother is talking about. Something about drowning and the father couldn't help him?" A. J. asks.

"My good God, she's talking about my son, who died in the river while fishing with my husband. My husband never got over it, hasn't left the house in years. You have to understand something about my mother, in case you haven't already noticed. She is in the beginning stages of Alzheimer's disease. We are looking into placing her in a nursing care home, but it's hard to find a good one at a good price. I'm sorry she babbled on with you. I just went to the Pound Stretcher Market to pick up some things for her. We don't like to leave her alone too long, just in case, you know?" says Gloria.

"Mr. Benson, I am truly sorry you have not been able to find your wife. I really don't know how to help you. I must get my mother changed and put down for her nappy, so could you please excuse us now?" requests Gloria.

"Oh, yes, of course, and I am sorry for the intrusion, thank your mother for me and tell her I'm sorry" asks Benson.

"Mr. Benson, my mother is standing right in front of you; she is still alive and can hear you. Perhaps you should tell her those things yourself." she adds.

Turning to Mrs. Mink, A. J. clears his throat and offers the old woman a nice little apology.

Turned back out onto Wallace Street, dejected and with no leads as to where his wife and son are, Benson heads for the corner pub he left a short while ago.

"Back so soon son? Did you find what you were looking for?" asks the barman.

"No, completely fucking waste of time, the old lady is dead and the old woman living there now is running on half a brain." the dejected detective states.

"Buy you a pint?" a voice from the other end of the bar asks.

About to order the same thing, A. J. looks up surprised at the figure at the end of the bar.

"Erin how did you…" an attempt to speak.

"Quite obvious you would end up in here." she states.

"She's not there, never has been." A. J. says.

"So what next my luv?" asks Erin.

"Let's have that Tennants and decide why our plan B is, alright?" he asks.

"Aye, now it's *our* plan B?" Erin quips.

"Yes Erin, it's our plan now" replies A. J. "will you help me?"

The first of several pints of Tennants Lager hit the bar. The cop and the barmaid sit and quietly chat. The more A. J. drinks, the more observant he becomes of the patrons drifting in and out of the pub. The days before Hogmanay are busy in the pub.

A. J. finds himself hoping to catch a glimpse of his wife, perhaps a face among the crowd of revelers. The once sharp eyed cop remains vigilant, watching, waiting at the bar near the door. Waiting for a miracle.

Chapter Fourteen

It was a typical winter night in Buffalo as Dr. Stratten drives into the parking lot of The Buffalo Chop House on Franklin Street in downtown Buffalo. A mere few minutes pass when Inspector Dave Alexander enters the same lot for the meeting.

"Good to see you Doc.", says the policeman as he shakes the hand of his friend.

"Likewise Dave. Feel like a steak? The filet here is fantastic. By the way, thanks for your call."

The two men adjust themselves in the seats and lean into each other.

"Doc, this is a fucking mess and I want you to know this information before anyone. I have located your brother. Well, sort of located him." he states.

A very youthful pubescent Jody Foster type arrives at the table to take the order. Both men order the large filet and a neat scotch. A lovely bottle of Joseph's Estate Pinot Noir from the wine region of Niagara-on-the-Lake is delivered to the table by the over-cheerful and smiling waitress.

"Tell me what's going on?" Dr. Stratten asks.

"Not much to tell, other than your brother is in Scotland at the moment."

"Scotland? What the fuck is he doing in Scotland?"

"Dunno for sure Doc, not yet anyway. Seems he left for there a few days ago, probably the day you came to his house to give him the psychiatrist referral."

"We know this how?" asks the doctor as Jody brings the Scotch and opens the bottle of Merlot.

"Passport Control reports your brother left Toronto on a British Airways flight the night before last. He connected in London to a domestic flight to Edinburgh Scotland."

"Why Scotland Dave, any idea?" the doctor asks.

"I was hoping you could shed some light on that Ken, any ideas on why he would go there?"

"The only Scottish connection, and this is a long shot, is that Angela was born there. I think A. J. mentioned that she had grandparents there still. Not quite sure, he never talked much about Angela in the past couple of years."

Inspector Alexander takes on his role of a seasoned interrogator and asks Dr. Stratten "Do you think he has found out where Angela and Jimmy are hiding, and he's gone to retrieve them? After all, she's gone with the kid and the place is cleaned out. The bank account she had at Marine Midland Bank was never touched. Her credit cards haven't been used since. They would need to be off somewhere where there was some support in place for them to live, don't you think?"

"What does Passport Control say about the movement of Angela and Jimmy? I never knew they even had current passports."

"Here's the hitch Doc, Passport Control have no record of Angela or Jimmy leaving the country."

"What about the bridges to Canada, they could have slipped over the river and into Canada couldn't they?"

"I checked with Customs on both sides Ken and they have no record of Angela or Jimmy entering Canada. I ran the plate on her car too through customs at the Peace Bridge, The Rainbow Bridge and Lewiston Bridge and no hit there either. Ken, from where I'm standing, I don't see where Angela and Jimmy ever left the area. Her car is accounted for, no clothes or belongings were ever taken from the house. The fucking chicken was still defrosting. Christ, the kids skateboard was still in the hall outside his room. They didn't take a thing with them."

The filet arrives. Jody pours the wine, pirouettes and retreats to other duties.

"What do you mean they never left the area?" Stratten asks.

"Doc, when A. J. first reported his wife and son, and the dog for that matter, missing, the Buffalo Police Department pulled out all stops to find them." He reports

"We reassigned officers from other divisions to assist in the search. After the house was completely examined by our seasoned officers, and forensics for that matter, we concluded that Angela and Jimmy may have been kidnapped. We thought it might have something to do with the El Hakim thing a year or so ago."

"Do you think that case has come back to haunt him" Ken asks of the officer.

"Hard to say for sure. Sure sounds like it though. Doc, how can two people, and one of them a young kid, disappear without a trace?" Dave asks. "We had officers stationed outside the airport, Amtrak and Greyhound terminals after they disappeared, and nothing. Not a sniff of them anywhere. It's like they, well, like they just evaporated or something, vanished. Sounds crazy doesn't it?"

"Yes the steaks are fine dear, bring us another scotch." the doctor orders from the returning waitress.

"Ken, as you know, our department had officers investigating this disappearance at every level. We checked and double checked School, recreation and sports centers, and anywhere Jimmy might have had some activity. Christ we had the goddamn Scoutmaster in the station all day, thinking that there was some kind of connection between him and Jimmy or between him and Angela. Nothing materialized out of that either." he states.

"Dave, I am alarmed that my brother has gone all the way to Scotland to look for his family and we don't even know that they're over there at all" Dr. Stratten explains.

"I'm very alarmed as well." states Alexander.

The men finish their steaks and enjoyed some of the wine when Dr. Stratten leans over to Dave, and very abruptly provides Alexander with some alarming diagnosis.

"Dave, the condition my brother is suffering from is Post-Traumatic Stress Disorder. I've been treating him at various levels of this syndrome for quite some time now, ever since the shooting at the crash test facility. This is an extremely debilitating condition that can occur after exposure to terrifying events like the one in the test facility." He says

"I am certain that my brother is experiencing the ordeal in the form of flashback episodes, nightmares and frightening thoughts. All through our many examinations since the shooting, I have noticed A.J.'s increasing tendency to reminisce about that event. He has developed an emotional numbness, depression, anxiety and outburst of anger."

"So he's really mentally ill?" asks Alexander.

"Very much so" the doctor replies.

"But why all of a sudden does he take off for Scotland? What's made him do this after all this time?"

"This is the part that disturbs me the most. In addition to experiencing depression, anxiety and anger, he has developed intense feeling of guilt because of the situation between him and Angela. Remember Dave, they were very much the perfect couple for a long time. Shit, you've known him since the early days on the force." Ken says.

"We used to undo a number of bras together in the old days too. Then he met Angela, and that all changed. He concentrated on being the best cop in town, stopped his bachelor habits and settled into family life."

"Dave, alcohol and other substance abuse can co-occur with the depression and other conditions in someone with this syndrome. Headaches and gastrointestinal complaints, chest pain, dizziness and discomfort in other parts of the body are common and were in fact the case with my brother." the doctor states.

"So what do we do now Doc? How can I help? Let's put some kind of game plan together." He says

"Dave, my brother is a very sick man. Mentally sick with a sick body. Something has caused this PTSD to remain unsatisfactorily treated. Even after all the debriefing that was done following his hospital stay, all the sessions he has had with me to treat him, he seems to be driven by something mad, unstable and perhaps even sinister." continues the doctor.

"Like what?" queries Alexander.

"It used to be believed that people who tend to dissociate themselves from the trauma were showing a healthy response. So we believed for a while that A. J. was improving. Research has now shown that people who experience dissociation may actually be more prone to PTSD and more likely to develop memory problems."

"So even when we find A. J., he may not remember anything to help us find Angela and Jimmy?" the cop asks.

"Exactly Dave, the problem just becomes convoluted because now we're dealing with someone with rapid memory loss, on top of all the other mental illness." Ken says.

"Ken I have some time owing me from holidays I didn't take. I'm going to take them now, get over to Edinburgh and get a fix on things. That sound alright with you?" Dave asks.

In obvious grateful agreement, Dr. Stratten tosses a Platinum Amex Card into Dave's direction.

"Take this Dave; get your flights, hotels, car rentals, meals and whatever you need. Put it on the card."

"Hey, no I can cover this. A. J.'s been a great guy to me over the years.

"No, you are truly a super guy Dave. To want to do this for me, for my brother and his family is very gracious and we all appreciate it. Man, you're giving up your holidays. Please Inspector, use the card. Live well and report to me often." Ken says.

"You want a little history lesson here Doc?"

"Sure Dave!"

"Many years ago, A. J. and I did a lot of range shooting. We got to making little bets on who would get the closest to blowing the head off or the heart out of the paper target. Your brother was always one of the best shots on the department. But I was better. In fact, that was the year I won the award for the best sharpshooter at Buffalo Police Department and went on to being in the state finals. After that your brother started to call me “Super Dave”, after a guy on some old television program. The nickname caught on pretty fast in the department too. The name Super Dave got shortened eventually to Super, then to Soop.” Dave advises.

“Well then Soop, get to Scotland and find my brother. But can you do one thing first before you go?”

“Sure Doc, anything”, Dave replies

“Dave, get the Platinum Card out and pay the dinner tab will you please? And leave Jody a nice tip.”

Chapter Fifteen

Additional passenger railcars had been coupled onto the local trains between Glasgow, Edinburgh and London to accommodate the gathering herds heading to Edinburgh for the Hogmanay celebrations. Only a few days away, the Edinburgh City Centre is in final preparations for the gala New Years Party in the Street.

The commuter train from Falkirk enters the Waverley Station in Edinburgh and spills its passengers into the waiting arms of family and friends. The long distance GNER and Virgin Railways trains from England make their presence known in the station by their massive locomotive engines and the brightly colored paint schemes of their passenger coaches, restaurant and sleeping coaches.

A. J. Benson and Erin leave through the front of the lead coach and head toward the terminal, and more purposely, Chester's Pub. Erin needs to check in and establish what her work schedule is for the next few days leading up to Hogmanay.

Erin pulls A. J. a pint of bitter before she heads out behind the bar to a staff area where the holiday schedules are posted.

"Cheers Erin." an appreciative A. J. says.

"Cheers back." she replies. "Back in a couple of minutes, OK?" she adds.

Pondering the events of the last couple of days has A. J. in a very contemplative mood. He reflects on his decision to come to Scotland to find Angela and Jimmy. He reflects on his health and his alcoholism. He reflects on his career, or what's left of it. He reflects on the wife and son he once had.

He is preoccupied with the thought of his new comrade Erin, her ability to make him feel good, her indisputable caring for him and her magnificent love making ability.

Most disturbing to him at the moment however, is the fact that A. J. and Erin were not able to even get s sniff where Angela and Jimmy might be in Scotland. The Falkirk connection was anything but that. No clue or trace of his family exists in the little town where Angela's heritage once thrived.

Chapter Sixteen

Police protocol around the world requires a visiting officer to make his presence known to the local authorities when doing investigations within their jurisdiction.

The Lothian and Borders Police Headquarters in Edinburgh Scotland are housed in a magnificent castle like edifice. The sleek black cab that Officer Dave Alexander hired at Edinburgh Airport enters the courtyard where security checks the arriving visitors. Cleared from this point, the cab delivers Alexander at the front entry to the building. He makes his way; carry on bag in hand, to the main information desk in the lobby.

"Good morning sir, may I help? Asks a female constable behind the counter.

"My name is Dave Alexander, from the Buffalo New York Police Department. I am in Edinburgh investigating the disappearance of an individual and would like to register my attendance in your jurisdiction.", he reports to the officer.

"Welcome to Edinburgh Officer." she says "Please be seated here and I'll advise the Chief Constable."

Dave feels he has done the right thing to announce his presence here, even though the investigation he is on is not a sanctioned or official investigation by the Buffalo Police Department. He feels confident in asking the Lothian and Borders Police for some assistance in this matter as well.

"Officer" the voice echoes from across the lobby "Come in sir. My name is Chief Constable Scott Goodbrand. Welcome to Edinburgh sir. Have you been here before?" he asks

"No Chief, my first time to Scotland." he replies.

"Officer Alexander is it? Very Scottish name you have sir, any local connection?" he asks.

"Not to my knowledge Chief, but yes, it is a Scottish name but my parents were both born in the States." He replies.

"Well then, what can we do for you sir?" he queries.

"I am here searching for another police officer, a friend of mine on the Buffalo Police Department. He's suffering from Post traumatic Stress Syndrome. He was shot taking part in an operation a year or so ago and has never recovered mentally from it. U. S. Customs Passport Control has him entering your jurisdiction on a flight from Heathrow where he connected from his British Airways flight from Toronto."

"What's the issue here?" asks Goodbrand.

"The issue here sir, is that A. J., his name is A. J. Benson, is over here looking for a wife and son who disappeared from their home several months ago."

"Seems pretty fundamental, what is your role here then Officer Alexander?"

"My role here is to find A. J. and bring him home so he can obtain the medical and psychiatric care he needs. His brother is a doctor, and has referred him to a Psychiatrist. That's when he left for Scotland. His wife is from near here, little place called Falkirk."

"Aye, Aye Falkirk, two good football clubs there. So you figure that's where he is?" asks Inspector Angus.

"Not sure just yet sir, but there is something troubling his brother and me, about the investigation into his wife's disappearance." Dave says.

"And that is?" he asks.

"There exists no reason to believe that his wife and son have ever left the Buffalo area. The Buffalo Police conducted a thorough investigation at the time, even had A. J. strapped into the lie detector." Alexander reports.

"Did he pass the polygraph?" asks the Chief Constable.

"Flying colors sir, no reason to think that Officer Benson had anything to do with his wife or son disappearing like they did." He replies.

"Help me here sir. What is the real issue here? It doesn't seem like any crime is being committed here and this man looking for someone who isn't here only means he doesn't know that they're not here." States the Inspector.

"Chief, with due respect sir, I feel that my friend A. J. has lost his mind. He's a mental case sir. There is nothing to suspect his wife and son are here, or anywhere else for that matter. They simply disappeared." Alexander says.

"What about the case he was on when he was shot, anything there?" asks the Chief.

"No sir, no abduction, no ransom request. We've ruled out kidnapping. Our people conducted a thorough investigation into this incident and how it might have something to do with the disappearance. This man has a sick mind sir; I need to find him as soon as possible."

"Well Officer Alexander, other than noting in our ledgers that you are here on Police business, there is nothing more I can suggest. We appreciate you notifying us in the appropriate professional manner sir. However, having said that, should you need an introduction into any other jurisdiction outside of Edinburgh, I shall be pleased to forward It." offers the Chief.

"Thank you Chief."

"Call me Scott, you're not one of my men, so let's relax the formality shall we?" suggests the Inspector.

"Thank you so much Scott." Dave replies.

"Carry on sir. Do you need a drive to your hotel?" asks the Chief.

"Yes, that would be nice, but I don't want to trouble you." Alexander replies.

The Chief Constable rises from behind his massive oak desk and summons an officer to bring a car around for Office Alexander and deliver him to his hotel. Within minutes, the same officer that first received Dave in the lobby was behind the wheel of the blue and white Lothian and Borders police car.

"Good Day again sir." offers the constable.

"And you as well. Dave Alexander is my name" he says nervously.

"Yes, you told me already. My name is Constable Janet Angus. Where would you like to be delivered to sir?" she asks.

Constable Janet Angus is a tall beautiful woman with light skin and fabulous reddish blonde hair. She is dressed in her police uniform skirt, white shirt under a tight fitting four button jacket. Alexander is wondering how difficult it must have been to button the jacket up over her shapely body and bullet resistant Kevlar vest.

"Nice to meet you Miss. I was lucky to get booked at the Jury's Inn on Jeffrey Street on such late notice. This is not the best time to be trying to find someone here, needle in haystack, is it?" he asks.

"There is definitely no shortage of people in the city for Hogmanay. Who are you looking for?" she asks.

"A friend, a good friend for years and a fellow police officer. He's in ill health and his brother and I need to find him, and soon." He states.

The ride from the police headquarters to the hotel takes the two officers through the city and into the Old Town where the Edinburgh Castle comes in view. As they travel down the cobblestone streets, Alexander is noticeably worried how he will proceed to find his friend. Maybe a good nights rest will help him focus? Maybe a walk up the Royal Mile to the Castle will help?

Constable Angus moves her police vehicle to the front entrance of the Jury's Inn where Alexander thanks his beautiful driver for her time and wishes her well in her police career.

The pressure of the water hitting his back rejuvenates Dave Alexander to a point where he feels he has some energy. The room at the Jury's Inn is cozy, warm with a soft bed. He's not ready just yet for bed though. The shower has brought him back to life. Alexander dives into his case and retrieves maps of Scotland. He searches the maps for a geographic bearing on the Town of Falkirk. Alexander believes this is the best place to start to look for Benson, because it was his wife's home town.

Having now located the town on his maps, Dave investigates just how to get to Falkirk. The Jury's Inn on Jeffrey Street is directly across from the massive Waverley Train Station. Dave decides to dress and take a walk over to the station to check on train times to Falkirk. Feeling much better, he entertains the thought of having a couple of drinks while he is out. He will also take the opportunity to check out the area and generally get his bearings.

The weather is cool this day, windy but no snow greets Dave as he exits the Jury's Inn. He's thinking how nice it would be in Buffalo in December not to have snow. Buffalo receives many feet of snow blowing off Lake Erie. They call it lake effect snow, and it piles up nicely on the city streets making travel sometimes impossible.

City streets are filled with people wandering about the area. The immense celebrations and fireworks are tomorrow night and the city of Edinburgh is ready. Amusement rides line the streets near Waverley Station. It reminds Alexander of a fall fair at home. There are stands selling hot and cold drinks, sausages and even haggis. All the citizenry appear to be in party mode. Tomorrow night this entire area will be cordoned off and entrance gained by ticket only.

Crossing the Waverley Bridge, he sees a huge Ferris wheel in a park overlooking a valley where an ice skating rink has been installed. Dave strolls down Princess Street and is overwhelmed at the sight of Edinburgh Castle. High above the city, the castle is fully lit with hundreds of spot lights shining on its edifice.

Dave is energized by the cool Scottish air and continues his stroll, taking in the sites and contemplating what the coming days will bring. A familiar sign soon comes into view. What could be more American than the Hard Rock Café on George Street? Dave is greeted by a lovely lassie named Karen, who seats him at the bar.

His bartender is Jake and soon learns that Jake grew up on the Canadian side of the Niagara River in a place called Bethel, near the City of Port Colborne on Lake Erie. It's only 30 minutes from Buffalo, New York. Alexander enlightens Jake on the standing in the National Hockey League and the Buffalo Sabres Hockey Team. Growing up near Buffalo, there was always the opportunity to go 'across the river' into the states to see major league sports and drink the cheaper American beer.

Dave grows tired after his break at the Hard Rock and decides to head back to the Jury's Inn for a good night sleep. As soon as he reaches the outer door of the bar, he is met with what many people around the world know Great Britain for best. Rain is pounding down on the city streets and all who occupy them. Last year, the entire Hogmanay celebration and fireworks were cancelled due to bad weather like this combined with high winds.

Dave quickens his pace as he becomes utterly soaked to the skin. Half way across the Waverley Bridge he sees the entrance to the train station. He decides to take the short cut from this entrance to that which is adjacent to his hotel.

The detour leads him through the great hall of the train station.

He stops in the busy abyss to view a direction sign. Dave looks around to get a fix on where he is and begins again, up the stairs which carry him over idling locomotives. The door exiting to Jeffrey Street is in sight.

At this moment he realizes he did not enquire about the train schedule to Falkirk. Dave wipes his brow and turns his direction back into the station.

Dave descends the stairs against the flow of people trying to go up the same flight of stairs. Approaching is a couple walking arm in arm, with noticeable difficulty in maneuvering the stairs. In an effort to avoid these people and give them an unobstructed climb, Dave moves out of the way, but not in time. He collides shoulder to shoulder with the man. The couple spins around like a top and come to a dead halt along the hand rail.

"I'm very sorry folks." Dave offers the couple.

The man lifts his head, looks at Dave directly in the eye and says "No problem."

The look of horror, shock and delight embraced the faces of both men.

"Soop? Is that you Soop?" asks a wobbly A. J.

"A. J. goddamn it man, what are you doing here?"

"Erin, this is my friend Dave Alexander, from back home in Buffalo." A. J. begins.

"Nice to meet you Dave." Erin says.

He does not reply to her greeting.

"Ya, ok, why are you here A. J? Christ, your piss drunk aren't you?

The trio moves up the stairs into the wider hallway inside exit door.

"So are you on holidays Dave or what?"

"Oh yes, I'm on my fucking holiday alright, but I'm using my holiday time to look for you. Your brother has been frantic since you left. He found your little note. Very mysterious aren't you and why Edinburgh?" Alexander demands.

"I don't like your tone." Erin says.

"Fuck you, I don't like yours either." right back to her.

"A. J. we need to get you back to the states." he says.

"But I'm not done here, I need to find Angela and Jimmy and I'm not leaving until I do find them."

"What makes you think they are here at all?" asks Alexander.

"The day that they disappeared, the phone in our den was off the hook. When I listened to it, I could hear an announcement about time and the weather in the Highlands. So by this I know that Angela and Jimmy are here, somewhere in Scotland." A. J. says.

"A. J. for months you never did a thing to find them, why now?" Dave asks.

"I suppose its guilt, plain simple guilt." He says.

"A. J. and I have a plan, so don't you worry." injects Erin.

"So what plan do you have A. J.?" asks Alexander, still not responding to Erin.

"Erin and I are going to find them. We've already been to Falkirk and they're not there. So we're going to look for them somewhere else."

"Where somewhere, this is a big fucking country, where are you going to look?" said Dave. "How do you know they're in Scotland? And if they are, do they want to be found? Do they A. J? Well come on man, give me some answers, what the fuck is this all about? Tell me man! Tell me why you slipped away like a cat in the night on this bullshit expedition? I've checked every possible nook and cranny for them A. J. There is nothing to lead us here, so what the fuck is this all about? They've never left the States! Never. You know this don't you?"

Eerie silence envelopes Waverley Station. Suddenly the thousands of passengers making their way in and out of the station make no noise at all. There is no sound from the diesel locomotives.

Taxicab horns become silent. No announcements are made on the public address system. The air inside of the station becomes cool. The entire place becomes silent. Dead silent.

An explosion rocks the station!

Chapter Seventeen

When someone with mental illness ignores his diagnosis and leaves the condition untreated, there eventually will be an internal detonation within the person. Like a spontaneous combustion, the person will erupt like a volcano. Uncontrollable anger is a major by-product of untreated PTSD. Erin and Dave are about to experience an eruption like never before.

Without notice A. J. begins swinging his fists at his friend and pulls him onto the ground where he begins to kick at him. Erin tries to intercede but is hit repetitively and thrown to the ground. A crowd begins to gather around the volcano.

A. J. has a complete loss of intellectual capacity as to where he is or who he is. He goes about striking anyone who comes near him. He turns again on his friend, then again on Erin, wildly beating them around the face and kicking when he cannot land a punch.

The scene is ugly and bloody as the Lothian and Borders Police arrive at the station. Erin appears unconscious on the floor of the terminal while Dave Alexander is sitting slumped on the floor against the stair rail.

"Halt! Police!" an order is shouted out.

A. J. paces like a caged animal, pacing back and forth just waiting for someone else to attack him. His arms are outstretched, his fingers moving wildly in and out. His head spins frenziedly around, his eyes not making contact with anyone. He shivers and quakes in his own footsteps.

"This is Lothian and Borders Police speaking, I need you to get down on both knees with your hands on the floor!" a policeman shouts.

More police arrive. Paramedics arrive but are held at bay until the situation is controlled. Passengers in the terminal are herded well away from the explosion.

"This is your last chance sir, get down on your knees and put both hands flat on the floor! Now sir!" as the order is given again.

It becomes imperative that the injured receive treatment as soon as possible. Time is of the essence in the treatment of head wounds. Dave, Erin and several others need immediate treatment.

The temperature in the place is now feverish.

"One last time, down on your knees now!" order the policeman.

A. J. Benson continues to pace in front of the police officers, then in a desperate bid he reaches into his jacket pocket. The police draw their weapons and take aim.

"No stop! He's a cop" offers Alexander.

Benson withdraws his hand from his pocket and takes aim at the wall of police that have now surrounded the area.

The order to shoot was silent. A police officer high on the steel girder above the situation takes quick and accurate aim at A. J. In a millisecond, the highly decorated Buffalo Police Detective is rendered immobile on the dirty wet floor of Waverley Station.

The officers who were aiming at Benson just a few minutes ago are now at his side, securing the scene and assessing the damage. Paramedics arrive and begin to treat Benson. The lead officer is concerned. As the paramedics perform their duties, the officer is searching A. J.'s clothing for a gun.

"There's no fucking gun!" a terrified Erin screams.

"She's right officer." says Alexander "I saw no gun!"

Officers and paramedics remove Erin and Dave Alexander to an area away from the shooting and begin their questioning. Paramedics treat Erin's facial injuries at the rear of the emergency ambulance in preparation to transfer her to hospital. Dave Alexander is still bleeding, is dazed and stunned but feels it more important to speak with the investigating officers before he is taken to the hospital.

"What can you tell me about this Mr. Alexander?" asks Chief Goodbrand.

"My friend there, his name is A. J. Benson. He's a fellow cop from Buffalo New York. He's here looking for his wife and son who left him with no forwarding details of any nature." Dave replies with as much information in one short breath as he could.

"Where is his wife now, why isn't she here?" asks the Chief Constable.

"He never found them. He met Erin, the girl in the other ambulance there, and by the sounds of it they had looked for his wife and son but found no clues." reports Alexander.

"What sparked this episode here sir?" asks Inspector Good brand.

"My friend is suffering from Post Traumatic Stress. He was shot on the job. I am here on behalf of his brother, who is also his doctor. He has tried to help A. J. deal with his condition. He never dealt with it."

"Why not?"

"Simple sir, he's a cop. You know how we are, stubborn most time, especially about ourselves? We don't like doctors and especially don't like bad news about ourselves, especially when it can affect your status on the police department. You know how we are Inspector Good brand, don't you?" he asks.

"Yes sir" he says dismissively. "Right then, so we have this U. S. policeman, looking for his family assisted by someone he just met, and then he beats his best friend and the new girlfriend in the train station, pulls out a gun that wasn't there and is shot by our Special Weapons Unit? Have I got that right so far sir?" he asks of Alexander.

"That's it in a nutshell. There is no gun. He would not have been able to bring a weapon to Scotland." says Dave.

Dave Alexander does not want to tell the Scottish cop about his suspicions about where Angela and Jimmy really are. He doesn't know exactly where they are, but has a sick feeling in his gut that cops get when something in a case just not make sense.

"Alright" says the Inspector, "let's get you to the infirmary as well and look at this situation later. Your friend is under arrest for public nuisance, threatening, battery and a number of other charges. He's not likely to be going home soon."

"He's a sick man Chief, don't forget that. What happened here is A. J.'s total mental meltdown. It is not something criminal. I know this man, I worked with him in the field, and he's a good cop, the ultimate cop. He's worked his way up from nothing to be one of the top homicide investigators in New York State."

"In that case sir, I presume you're pleased our marksmen only wounded your friend? You see sir, they did hear you tell them he was a police officer. Perhaps you've saved his life by that." says the Inspector.

Alexander is seated on the cushion in the back of the emergency ambulance as it takes him to the same hospital as Erin and the others strangers. The Royal Infirmary hospital on Lauriston Place is a five minute drive from Waverley.

Alexander only has a few minutes to ponder just how to tell Dr. Stratten of these events when he calls him. The ambulance makes the wide turn from Forest Road onto Lauriston and into the infirmary. Police vehicles follow the ambulance to the entrance to the emergency room.

Paramedics are fastidious as they hold onto the wound dressings covering Alexander's face as he is walked slowly through the doors of the emergency infirmary and onto a waiting cot.

"Mr. Alexander, my name is Doctor Kremer, I'm your doctor."

"Tell me what happened here" he says as he begins to remove the dressings.

"It's kind of a weird situation Doctor Kremer. I am a police officer from the States. I located the man I was looking for and he attacked me and others." reports Dave.

"Is he a bit of a mental case?" he asks

"No doc, he's a good friend but he suffers from a mental disorder that prevents him from understanding reality at the moment." said Dave.

The removal of the bandages exposes a bruised and torn face, a broken nose and lacerations around the eyes.

Blood is streaming from the deep gash that crosses the back of his head from the tip of his right ear to the base of his neck.

"Let me have a local syringe please." asks Dr. Kremer.

"Xylocaine, yes Doctor" replies the emergency room nurse.

"Mr. Alexander, I'm giving you an injection of xylocaine to let you relax while we mess about with your arm. You will need a bit of minor surgery to repair the damage to your face and head."

Your nose is broken and needs to be set and your right cheek bone is shattered. I will do the initial surgery, but follow up will be required when you get back to the states."

"You sure this chap was your friend?" the doctor asks.

"He's a troubled man doc, how is he doing?" asks Dave

"Listen my friend; we have enough damage to you to be troubled about for now. I will check with the other emergency team in a while to see how your friend is." offers the doctor.

Tall with a full head of black wavy hair, Dr. Kremer is a young, mild mannered man with an unmistakable South African accent. He has a gentle but firm bedside manner.

Dr. Kremer orders the injection to be administered then offers Alexander a "good night sir."

Chapter Eighteen

Chief Constable Scott Goodbrand is not amused as the officers walk fast stride toward the locked infirmary ward.

His mobile phone call to the headquarters of the Buffalo New York Police Department was not well received.

Goodbrand is enlightened by his counterpart in Buffalo during the ensuing telephone conversation that neither Benson nor Alexander are on official police business in Edinburgh.

Leanne Ronalds is the Chief of the Detective Division and Investigation Services for the Buffalo Police Department. She is shocked to hear the news of what materialized at Edinburgh's Waverley Train Station. She verifies that Dave Alexander and A. J. Benson are ranking members of the BPD. She also confirms that no international investigation is under way in the matter of A. J. Benson and that Officer Alexander is not on official police business in Edinburgh.

"Well then sir, I must inform you we have an official international incident." says Chief Constable Goodbrand.

"It appears that way doesn't it Inspector?"

"I don't fully understand what Officer Benson is doing in Scotland but certainly Officer Alexander is blameworthy and will face charges as a result. My people here will continue to investigate his movements. This is very serious. We certainly don't appreciate your officer arriving in Edinburgh and conducting an investigation under false pretense." The Inspector advises Chief Ronalds.

Goodbrand continues "Several people were hurt in this incident, including a woman who works in the pub at Waverley Station. She apparently was a friend of your officer Benson and was seen with him in Falkirk making use of the local pub. They were also investigating something.

I have a copy of a complaint lodged by a woman in Falkirk detailing how your Officer Benson went to her mother's house and questioned her about some people she never knew. The name they were looking for was Angela Forgie, evidently the wife of A. J. Benson." says the Inspector.

"Benson's wife went missing along with their son about two years ago. There was never a trace of them." reports Ronalds.

"What is the link here Chief? What is stimulating these two officers to be in Scotland stirring up shit?" asks Goodbrand. "You cannot have your officers arrive in my jurisdiction and deceive my office of their intentions."

Chief Ronalds can sense the frustration in the voice of her counterpart in Scotland. She is also seething at this situation.

"Chief Goodbrand, let me assure you that these officers were not on official police business in Scotland. In fact, Officer Benson is on sick leave at the moment. I want to extend my sincere apologies to the Lothian and Borders police for this terrible and inexcusable chain of events. I am going to pledge to you that a full investigation will take place on our side of the Atlantic." Ronalds says, "And we will reopen and extend our investigation into the disappearance of Benson's family."

The officers arrive and open the locked infirmary room holding A. J. Benson to find the patient asleep. He has been sedated to ease the pain from the injuries to his shoulder. Not willing to wait for answers, the two junior officers aggressively agitate the wounded officer. They stimulate him to an awakened state.

Benson is clearly unhappy and in a great deal of agony.

"Mr. Benson, my name is Chief Constable Scott Goodbrand; I am with Lothian and Borders Police Department here in Edinburgh. I'd like to ask you a few questions." the Inspector asks.

"I'm not in the mood to talk actually." said A. J.

"That is unfortunate for you sir. I am in the mood to talk, and since you are under arrest on several charges, and the guest of our lock up here, I suggest you prepare yourself for a little discussion." He adds.

Two more officers from the Lothian and Borders Police join Inspector Goodbrand.

"Right then Mr. Benson, let's get right to it shall we? What the bloody hell are you doing here in Scotland?" the Inspector demands.

"I'm on official police business here, looking for some missing persons" A. J. says.

"Funny thing that."

"What's funny?" Benson asks.

"It's peculiar that your Chief of Detectives in Buffalo doesn't know anything about you being here. He certainly knows nothing of any investigation. Do you think he would know about an ongoing investigation Mr. Benson? Do you think a man in his position would know where his men are and what they're investigating?" he asks.

A shrug by Benson indicates his feeling of discomfort at the questions he knows will follow.

"Well then sir, tell me what a police officer on sick leave hopes to accomplish by asking questions about his missing wife?"

"I am looking for my missing wife and son. Through a tip of sorts, I believe them to be hiding here in Scotland. My wife is from Falkirk originally and...."

"Oh yes, yes, yes." The Chief Constable interrupts "Mrs. Mink, the lovely old lady in Falkirk. Her daughter registered a complaint about you when you left the house. Seemed she really didn't believe you were there in that intoxicated state on police business." He says.

"The Wallace Street address is where my wife's family once lived Inspector. I thought this was a good place to start looking for her. Her grandparents are dead now and the old lady didn't know where my wife and son could be" says A. J.

"Were they ever there?" asks the Constable in the room.

"Why would you ask an old lady all these questions, put her on the spot when she has no memory to speak of?" the third officer asks.

"How the fuck did I know she had no memory? The old girl was telling me all kinds of things. How did I know she was Looney?" quips A. J.

"Just because someone has signs of Alzheimer or Dementia, does not qualify them to be Looney sir, in fact, if anyone is Looney here, I suggest it could be you. What kind of sick leave are you on Mr. Benson?" asks the Chief Constable.

"Stomach problems." A. J. replies.

"Stomach problems have anything to do with that healed scar on your head?" he asks.

"No that's a scar from an old accident, nothing to be alarmed about." says A. J. "reluctant to talk about the gunshot wound from the Brent Carl case.

Goodbrand, wanting to wrap up this questioning moves close to the bed now where A. J. Benson lingers. He moves a chair and sits face to face with the injured policeman.

"Mr. Benson, or should I say Officer Benson, are you familiar with the term PTSD?" asks the Chief.

"No." he replies flatly.

"Let me help you in that case sir. It's a term, coined in the U. S. by psychiatrists and psychologists to characterize the mental condition of someone who has undergone a life threatening experience. Sound familiar now?" he asks.

"Yes" A. J. replies, "But I don't have that! I'm fine."

"Yes my friend you do, so sayeth your Chief. She tells me you are off work on a mental health sick leave, ordered by your doctor. She also tells me that he is going to have a look at the missing person's case of your wife and son. Does this please you?" asks the Chief.

A. J. is clearly stunned by this revelation. The blood drains from his face and he becomes pale and motionless, his mouth open as if to catch flies.

"Of course I'm pleased, why wouldn't I be?" he grunts.

"I don't know sir; you tell me why you wouldn't be pleased?"

The meeting is over without a reply from A. J. Benson. A police constable locks the door and takes his seat outside the room guarding the visiting prisoner. The three officers proceed down the long narrow hallway to the post surgery ward.

Chapter Nineteen

Recurrent nightmares are the most defining symptom of Post Traumatic Stress Disorder. These nightmares disturb sleep and alter daytime behavior in the afflicted. The frequency of PTSD nightmares increases with the severity of trauma, hostility, poor health habits, depression and poor coping skills. These nightmares are terrifying dreams in which worst fears are brought to life in convincing detail.

A. J. Benson has suffered from terrors of the night since he was a child. He experienced violent action filled dreams as a child, the result of experiencing the death of his father. The terror began the night after his father died in their home. A. J. was then a young boy of four.

The horror of his waking life caused him to dream about the circumstances of his father's death. The recurring vision of his mother holding the pillow over his father's unconscious body acted like a catalyst of sorts, a confirmation of A. J.'s worst fears being brought to life.

His father was dead.

These dreams soon turned into night terrors for the young A. J. He would no sooner fall asleep when nocturnal episodes of extreme terror and panic enveloped the child. He would wake up, confused and aroused. Blood curdling screams were often heard from his room. Other disorders arose. Somnambulism or sleepwalking became a regular experience.

His mother would hold A. J. during these episodes, cuddle him and keep him calm until his elevated heart rate fell and he once again drifted off into deep sleep.

Mrs. Benson never sought medical attention for A. J. in fear of being exposed as a murderer. The little family lived through the nightly horrors for years until Mrs. Benson married Mr. Stratten. Soon after, A. J. was presented with a little brother, named Kenny.

Being plagued with the nightmares as a child, A. J. never had the chance to fully recognize what they meant or how they affected him individually. He lived in fear of glancing toward the open door of his parent's bedroom.

He had only his mother to depend on due to his young age and lack of knowledge at the time. The nightmares and night terrors became less frequent when the happy Stratten family moved from the home where his father was murdered, and into a brand new home of their own.

Since his recovery from the shooting at the crash test facility, the night terrors increased in frequency. His first experience in a long time was that of being awake, but not in control of his body. He was sick with a fever following surgery to remove the bullet from his face. He appears in his mother's bedroom. He saw a black shadow pass the window and enter the room. Inside he was screaming and frantic, outside he knew that nothing was happening. Or was it? He was dreadfully afraid of more people coming into the room. He fought to wake up, terrified, and dreaming something awful was happening. Wake up, wake up, wake up, wake up, wake up.

He turned to face the thing and challenged it to go away. The thing was going to kill him. He tried to think the thing out of his mind but could not. The thing thumps his tiny body, batters his little head, and thrusts his small body toward the door. He brings himself to his feet, then turns again to face the thing. The thing is silent, quiet; eyes wide open, and tongue extended bleeding. The thing has been silenced and made quiet.

The tiny prisoner is released, shepherded to the sanctuary of his room, filled with model airplanes and plastic dinosaurs. The disturbing images cease. Mother is here now. All is well.

Chapter Twenty

Detective Chief Leanne Ronalds is a focused, tough career policewoman. Totally professional in every aspect of her personal and professional life, she does not suffer fools lightly. She has zero tolerance for bad cops and bad procedures.

Ronalds is under a great deal of professional pressure these days. While murders were down last year, the number of rape and robbery crimes has increased significantly. There were two hundred more bodily assaults last year than the previous year. The total violent crimes have been increasing for the past couple of years. Non violent crimes like burglary and larceny have decreased in recent years. Leanne is in complete control of her division and takes the statistics to heart. Her division deals with everything from homicide to forgery, gambling, prostitution, weapons and drug offences. Her division even deals with charges involving possession of burglary tools.

What her division is not used to dealing with are charges relating to her own officers especially when they have been charged with mischief and public endangerment in another country. Ronalds was involved as a detective in the initial missing person's case of Angela and Jimmy Benson. While not the lead detective on the case, she supervised every aspect of the investigation.

When a major investigation of this nature involved police officers, extra prudent care must be taken in the investigations stages.

Chief Leanne Ronalds was the officer who requested that A. J. Benson submit to lie detector tests with Buffalo Police polygraph specialists. Benson willingly accepted the invitation. Benson was forthcoming with information about his wife, his son, their movements and regular activities. He opened his home to investigators. Benson provided lists of his own personal contacts to the investigators in the hope some further information could be turned over from the contact.

Chief Ronalds was a sounding board of sorts with some of the more seasoned detectives on the force. Dave Alexander reported to her about the sexual activities of A. J.'s wife on several occasions. Apparently, word had spread fast and hard about Angela's desire to be bedded down by officers of the BPD. Nothing at the time of the original investigation led detectives to believe that A. J. Benson had anything to do with his wife and son's disappearance. After all, he passed the polygraph with flying colors.

In lieu of the results of the polygraph, Ronalds still felt she had to have Angela's movements investigated. Unofficial reports had surfaced about Angela's activities at local bar and with local cops. She worked very closely with the lead investigators of the case Jake and Lex Messer.

Jake and Lex are brothers, they joined the force the same day, obtained the same grades through training, shoot in the range with the same accuracy and are overall good thorough investigators. Any sensitive cases involving members of the force are usually handled by the Messer Brothers. It was Jake and Lex Messer who interviewed most of A. J.'s personal contacts.

Benson had an extensive list of personal contacts. He was involved in community groups, Boy's and Girl's Club Committees, Police Associations and The Buffalo Historical Society. He even found time to devote to a part time job of sorts with a local undertaker.

Everyone on his list was interviewed in detail. After all, this was a case involving the wife and son of a prominent Buffalo Police Officer.

Chief Leanne Ronalds on the other hand, along with Dave Alexander reopened the file on the Crash Test Facility in search for clues. Initially it was believed that there may be some Saudi connection to the disappearance of Angela and Jimmy Benson. This too was investigated to an exhaustive level but turned no new evidence. It seems that the Saudi circle was broken once El Hakim was shot and Brent Carl was taken into custody.

In light of the new revelations in Edinburgh, Ronalds decided to visit Attica prison to visit Brent Carl. Could some vendetta have been initiated through Carl from his prison cell?

Ronalds and Detective Emery Walter arrived at Attica New York at noon. They were received by prison officials who quickly escorted them to the interview cell of Block DD where they will be reacquainted with Brent Carl. The cell is small, with metal table and metal chairs in the middle of the grey painted concrete floor. A single cell door awaits the prisoner. Painted metal bars shield the room.

Brent Carl, known in prison simply as "Carlos" is one of very few white prisoners held there. Most are black or Hispanic. Most are from Metropolitan areas like New York City. Carlos has celebrity status in prison they discover. Carlos appears in a ridiculous long white T-Shirt with a large decal saying "ATTICA PRISON" and the line underneath "Season Ticket Holder."

"Thanks for dressing up for us Brent." says Chief Ronalds.

"Hey don't mention it. When I heard you were coming here yourself, I couldn't resist." he quipped.

"Let's cut the shit here Carlos." says Walter. 'The chief and I have some questions for you." He adds

"Well, I'm a little busy today." Carlos replies.

"Fuck you!" Walter replies with a heavy fist hitting the metal table with a bang.

"Ok, Ok, you made your point. Nice to see you again Chief, this guy your driver?" ask Carlos.

"You've slipped a long way down the pole from the old days haven't you Brent? Seems I remember you in some pretty fancy clothes driving some pretty fancy cars living in some pretty fancy homes with a real fancy wife. By the way, I hear your wife is fucking her way across the country with some young stud. You heard that too Brent?" asks the Chief.

"I don't really give a shit anymore to be honest with you. Yes, I got greedy but that's all." Replies Carl.

"No, that's not all." says Officer Walter, "People are dead and injured from your escapades sir."

“Yes, and my son was one of them.” replies Brent.

“What’s that?” asks the Chief and Emery at the same time.

The two officers seemed surprised at what Brent Carl is reporting. The effort to humiliate him about his past life and his wife had failed, but they seemed to hit a sore spot about Carl’s son for some reason.

“Tell me more about what happened to your son.” asks Chief Ronalds.

“I thought you knew. It happened about 6 months after I was registered as a guest at this shit hole.”

“We didn’t hear, go on, what happened?” replies Emery.

“My son decided to finally visit his old man, so set out with a couple of friends from Buffalo. Seems they only got a few miles up the interstate when his Lexus LX they were riding in blew a tire, veered off the interstate, crossed the median and hit a Shell Oil tanker head on coming from the other direction.”

“Sorry, I didn’t know.” replied Ronalds.

“My son’s body was so badly burned he was baked right onto the asphalt road surface. The wreckage of the tank truck rested on top of him and burned for an hour until it was extinguished. When the tow trucks finally removed the wreckage, his carbonized body was exposed, still smoldering. His head had been crushed coming through the windshield of the car and burned away. The investigating officers thought he had been decapitated. It was dark by this time so they asked the TV crews with their big lights to search the ditches for my son’s head. He had been all burned up. They never found any trace of my son’s head. He’s lying in his grave with no head. I couldn’t even attend his funeral. The poor kid has no head and it’s my fault.” Carl says tearfully.

“How horrible Brent, but our visit here has nothing to do with your son.” injects the Chief.

“Body removal arrived after crash photos were taken and I’m told they had to use a flat sided shovel to scrape my son’s body off the road. Like a burned mess being lifted from a frying pan. He was such a beautiful kid. He had nothing to do with my dirty deeds but he suffered in the end for it. His mother abandoned him to slut around with anyone she could. He was left on his own to fend for himself." a now sorrowful Brent Carl says.

"Brent, we need to ask you something, and perhaps you can answer truthfully. It's very important." asks Ronalds.

"What is it then?" replies Brent.

"The officer who investigated your car theft organization has had some trouble. His wife and son are missing. I know we spoke with you about this months ago, but for reasons we are not able to reveal right now, we are having a closer look at some of the cases that A. J. Benson was working on." reports Ronalds.

Brent Carl shuffles in his chair, looks directly at the two officers across the desk.

"Poor man. Isn't it a pity that his wife has disappeared along his son and his dog? Seems a bit like my situation doesn't it? My wife is gone and now my son. I have nothing to live for." Carlos boldly states with new defiance.

"Carl, do you know anything about the disappearance of Benson's family?" Ronalds demands.

"I know all about it." he states flatly.

In a split second, Carlos ejects from his metal chair and in another second tears his Attica Prison T-Shirt to shreds. The officers have no weapon, having been required to leave them at the prison office. Officers Ronalds and Walter jump from their seat in an attempt to subdue the now wild Carlos.

Carlos moves around the room ripping the shirt into long strands. The two officers try to corner the caged beast but cannot get close. They scream for assistance. The sound of the metal barred doors opening can be heard from down the hall.

In a flash, Carl coils the end of his shirt threads around his neck tightly. Instantaneously he knots the other end of the shirt around the cross bar of the cell. Ronalds and Walter pounce on Carl, which only prompts Carl to dive to the floor. He is suspended a mere foot or two from the cell floor, his neck nicely snapped.

Ronalds and Walter are thunderstruck. How could this have happened?

The officers are joined by prison guards, who try in vain to resuscitate their prisoner. They cut him off his T-Shirt sling and his body slumps to the floor. Ronalds thought that if he wasn't dead, the drop to the floor with neck injuries would probably have killed him. A death sentence.

"Anything registers with you as being a bit odd?" asks Ronalds of officer Emery Walter.

"Oh ya boss, loud and clear." Walter replies.

"Me too goddamn it" She replies "How did he know about the dog?"

Chapter Twenty-one

The only thing Dave Alexander can think about is getting out of Edinburgh. He always wanted to visit Scotland. Being admitted to hospital with head wounds was not his idea of the perfect holiday. Awake now in the locked infirmary, he is feeling much better since his face has been readjusted back to near its normal shape and his head has been repaired and stitched. He can't help thinking about the events of the past couple of days. He wonders how A. J. is. The Lothian and Borders Police have been very cagey on keeping the two men apart. Do they fear some type of conspiracy or organized deception?

Edinburgh Scotland is the most exciting place in the whole world to celebrate New Years. New York City's Time Square celebrations or the astonishing fireworks over the Sydney Harbor and Opera House in Australia pale by comparison to the festivities in Scotland. Edinburgh is by and large a safe place to live and to celebrate. The Royal Bank of Scotland sponsors the huge Hogmanay event in Edinburgh. If you are not one of the 125,000 people who have tickets for the event in the downtown core of Edinburgh, you just won't get in. Security is beyond tight. The Scottish people dignify Hogmanay with a two day holiday featuring heaps of drink and music. Stages are set around the downtown area. Ice skaters make good use of the rink assembled for the holiday in The Princess Street Gardens.

Alexander was quite aware of the time of year when he embarked on this trip. He was absolutely sure he would have difficulty in finding A. J. Benson. While Edinburgh is not a huge city, it does have its geographic restrictions. The city itself is set inland, amongst hills and valleys of ancient times. The Edinburgh Castle rises majestically above the rest of the city.

"Dave, this is Ken Stratten, what the fuck is going on over there?" the voice on the mobile phone says.

"More than I bargained for Ken, for sure. We've got big trouble. A. J. is in poor shape. He's had a bad time mentally over here." Dave says.

"So I hear my friend. I want you to know that I support what you tried to do. I am so grateful to you for finding A. J." Dr. Stratten says.

"I really didn't find him Ken. As much as I'd like to take credit for a real Sherlock Holmes deal here but I can't. I bumped into him in the train station. I simply bumped into him." Dave reports.

"It doesn't matter Dave. I've been made aware of what happened and recognize you're in a bit of a spot. Why did you tell the cops there you were on police business?" Ken asks.

"Courtesy only I guess. I figured if I needed their help, I would get it more readily if I was on official business. Now I'm fucked. I hear they are going to charge me later today with all kinds of shit. Probably lock me up in that fucking big castle over there." Dave says.

"Not quite Dave. I have spent the last twenty four hours or more convincing the Lothian and Borders Police Department to let you return to the States. I've got some connections with the State Department and that helped tremendously. I had to speak with the Crown Attorney of Edinburgh. He was ready to eat you alive, not to mention my brother. Dave, I had to promise them I would get you back here immediately and they would drop charges pending on you."

"How the fuck did you do that?"

"I'll tell you when you're back here. You will be contacted shortly by the police there and driven to Edinburgh Airport. You'll board a Continental Airlines flight there to New York. There, you'll connect to a flight to Buffalo/Niagara. Leanne Ronalds and I will pick you up." he says.

"Oh fuck, the boss is coming with you?" Dave asks reluctantly.

"Yes. Dave, there's something you have to know."

"What's that Ken?"

"She's on your side. They've looked into the missing person's case again. I spoke with Leanne this morning. It seems that Brent Carl, has killed himself in jail. Before he hung himself with the boss and Emery Walter as an audience, he basically admitted he had something to do with Angela and Jimmy's disappearance" Ken reports.

"Well I'll be fucked. Do you believe it Ken?" asks Dave.

"Brent Carl was always a sly fucker you know. I don't believe it for a minute. Dave, just get back here in one piece alright? We'll chat tomorrow night when you get in."

"Ken, what about A. J.? When is he coming home?" Dave asks.

"We're working on this too my friend, but time will tell. Just get back here. We'll work it out." said Ken.

Chapter Twenty-two

The car arrived at the Infirmary late in the afternoon of New Years Eve. Constable Janet Angus has been put in charge of Office Alexander and made responsible for his safe and expeditious delivery to the Edinburgh Turnhouse Airport.

"Good afternoon sir." she says with a huge smile.

"To you as well. It's Constable Angus right?" asks Dave.

"Actually, it's First Class Constable Angus sir." She replies.

"Are you driving me to the airport First Class Constable Janet?" He asks with a laugh.

"Yes, I am your chauffeur sir. I would love to see your part of the world some day. Do you think the Chief Constable would mind me accompanying you all the way to Buffalo? Would you like that?" she asks. "I could deliver you right to your Chief." She says with a wink and a warm smile. "It's unfortunate that they didn't make this part of the deal to get you out of Scotland."

"To tell you the truth Janet, I'd rather not be here in the first place, but if I have to get home right away, I'd be glad to have you as a traveling companion." He says. "You are welcome anytime you would like to come to visit me. There's so much to see and do. We could visit Niagara Falls; it's only a few minutes from where I live. Toronto is a fantastic place too and only an hour or so away. I would love to take you up the CN Tower." He says.

"What is a CN Tower?" She asks.

"The CN Tower is the tallest free standing structure in the world and there's a fantastic view from the outside observation deck. You'll love it. On one level part of the floor is Plexiglas so you can stand and look straight down to the ground. It's very scary. You may need a big strong cop to hold on to." Dave says.

"Cheers then." She says, cutting him short on his feeble attempt at flirting, "Let's get you out to the car and make our way to the airport shall we? It's not far and won't take us long to get there. We need to make a stop at the Jury Inn to pick up your personal effects on the way." Constable Angus says.

"I barely had a chance to unpack the bag." Dave says.

Chapter Twenty-three

Ever since she moved to Edinburgh, Erin loved to venture out onto the 10th floor rooftop of her Jeffrey Street flat. From this vantage point she can clearly view Edinburgh Castle and the Old Town. In the other direction she overlooks Waverley Station and can see the lights of the Princess Street shopping district and the massive Balmoral Hotel.

The rooftop is the perfect perch for her as she acquires pleasure from cans of Tennants Lager in quiet tranquility. She has no family nearby and tends to want to stay by herself in solitude. The only noise she hears from her roost is the rumbling of the diesel engine locomotives moving in and out of Waverley.

She acknowledges to herself that she will not be able to work at Chester's Pub at Waverley until the bruising on her face has faded. She is not anxious to return to Waverley either. The terror of the last couple of days remains still unambiguously on her mind.

Erin reflects on how quiet the evening is, which surprises her because it is New Years Eve, Hogmanay in Edinburgh. The City is ready for the worlds most festive New Years Celebration. Erin rests comfortably on an ancient red velour sofa, brought up to the roof by her neighbors from across the hall. Erin hasn't seemed the neighbors since she returned from hospital. Four young men share that adjacent apartment. Two of the men are Canadians, working in the restaurant business; one is a South African working as a photographer and the other, a local of Arab Tunisian descent whose employment she is unsure of.

Erin paces the roof, looking out over the street below. Holiday merry makers are winding their way in and out of the trendy restaurants and pubs that line the street. She is envious for a life so enjoyable. A. J. Benson is on her mind this night as the New Year approaches. She yearns to be with him to welcome 2006 but acknowledges the reality of the situation with him. He is not with her, but rather in a locked hospital ward under police guard, a contemplation that causes her a lot of anguish.

Erin attempted to visit A. J. before she left the same infirmary emergency room but to no avail. The Lothian and Borders Police refused to entertain her request to see him. Instead, they cleared her of any involvement in the explosion at Waverley, called a cab and sent her home.

Erin's decision to end her life was well thought out. She would use the loftiness of her building to her advantage. She hoped that being ten stories above the sidewalk was enough to kill her.

It was.

First to come to Erin's rescue was the owner of the baked potato shop on the street level of her building. He was concerned about having her body removed immediately because she lay directly in front of door to his business. Blood streaming from her fractured skull ran down the sloped sidewalk. Sections of white brain matter ooze from the crater in her head and out of her shattered nose.

Her arms and legs are dislocated to that resembling a contortionist at a side show. The pressure of the collapsed skull has caused her eyes to explode and detach from their sockets.

Bad for business for the potato guy.

It is genuinely sad that her lonely life and sudden death have been condensed into being an inconvenience.

Chapter Twenty-four

Constable Angus maneuvers the Lothian and Borders unmarked police vehicle across the George IV Bridge and onto High Street. Alexander watches as keenly as a tourist as they pass the High Court of Justiciary and Edinburgh City Chambers. She signals a turn as they pass the former home of John Knox, the Presbyterian preacher who launched and directed the Scottish Reformation in 1555.

Turning onto Jeffrey Street they come to a halt at a wall of flashing blue, white and red lights. Paramedic ambulances and police vehicles block the sloped street and ultimately the passage to the Jury Inn.

Officers Angus and Alexander abandon their vehicle to check what has happened. The two seasoned officers approach the uniformed policeman at the scene in front of the potato shop. Janet identifies herself to the officer. Wanting to stay out of the limelight, Alexander does not identify himself.

"Jumper", says the uniformed officer.

"It's the time of year don't you think? Janet says to the officer.

"Normally yes, but not in this case I'm afraid. The jumper here is the woman who was attacked in the train station the other day. The poor soul. Just look at her. She must have been so depressed." the officer states.

"Janet, can we just get the hell out of here please?" a visibly shaken Alexander demands.

Chapter Twenty-five

Dr. Etienne Kremer has spent the last three days in the Infirmary and is preparing himself now to leave for the night. He plans to enjoy Hogmanay Celebrations with friends and co-workers. Before he leaves, he has a meeting with Chief Inspector Scott Goodbrand of Lothian and Borders Police, Assistant Crown Attorney Pat Rushton, Hospital Superintendent Martin McQueen and Detective A. J. Benson. The three will meet in Superintendent McQueen's office on the main floor of the sprawling hospital building.

The mood is quite somber as the participants arrive. There is none more serious than A. J. Benson, the last to arrive.

"Mr. Benson, I want you to meet some people who are here to help you." says Dr. Kremer.

This is the first time in days that A. J. Benson has heard anyone say they wanted to help him. He is taken aback by this statement and perks up to listen for more.

"Mr. Benson, this is Edinburgh Assistant Crown Attorney Patricia Rushton. She is here to advise you on your legal standing here in Edinburgh. You already know Chief Inspector Goodbrand and Mr. McQueen from our hospital management." He says.

Crown Attorney Rushton is a no nonsense type of professional. She is an elegant middle aged woman who even late in the afternoon, looks and seems as fresh as if she just began work in the morning. She has a file folder under her arm that measures at least a foot thick. The contents of this folder intrigue A. J. "How could I have such a large file having only been here for a couple of days?" he thought.

When Miss Rushton finally speaks, it is with clarity, influence and authority.

"Inspector Benson, I am here to advise you of your standing, or lack of standing, here in Edinburgh. As a result of lengthy deliberations with your brother, other doctors, the U. S. State Department your FBI and the Edinburgh Crown Attorney we are here to make you an offer. This is an offer that you will sign and by doing so promise to abide by its contents." she says.

"Of course madam." replies A. J. He fears the worst. He fears once he recuperates he will be dragged off to some dungeon of a jail beneath Edinburgh Castle and left to rot like some floater under the Peace Bridge.

She continues "Officer, throughout the day, a case has been made in your favor based on testimony by your brother, Chief Ronalds and many others that you are suffering from a debilitating mental condition. In light of this, we, the Crown Office of Edinburgh, the Lothian and Borders Police Department, your own doctor, FBI and others are advising you that you will be released from this institution to return to the United States. You are being deported from Great Britain on order from this Government. We are in no mood to prosecute you based on what we know about you. This deportation, if you accept it, is final. You will not be allowed to enter Great Britain for the rest of your life." She says.

The statements of fact come fast and furious from Miss Rushton. She speaks directly to Benson, eye to eye, and he respects that. He senses some sort of compassion however, something of an understanding in her voice.

"Make no mistake about this deportation order Officer Benson. It is the same type of deportation order that we swear out for citizens of other countries that have run afoul of our laws. Sir, this deportation from Great Britain is now in effect and will be enforced in due course. The actual deportation back to the United States will not happen however, until you have undergone some preliminary psychiatric examinations and your shoulder wound has healed sufficiently for you to travel. Do you understand this sir?" says the Attorney.

"Mr. Benson, you need to help yourself here and accept what you've done and get some help for your problems." interjects the Chief Inspector.

Benson turns to acknowledge Miss Rushton and Inspector Goodbrand. "Yes I understand, completely."

"Furthermore you must promise to undergo psychiatric treatment once you arrive back in the states. Is that clear?" Miss. Rushton says.

"Alright yes, I'll look into when I get home, thank you." replies A. J.

"Don't be a fucking asshole here Benson, we're cutting you a colossal break here." says Chief Inspector Scott Goodbrand. "We're not asking you to go home and maybe take a tablet. We're demanding you abide by the contract you are about to sign." He says loudly.

Dr. Kremer feels the need to defend his patient.

"A. J., your brother has arranged for you to be admitted to the Erie County Medical Centre upon your return. Once home, you will be admitted to the Psychiatric Unit where you will receive comprehensive psychiatric assessment and treatment. We recognize you are a decorated and dedicated police officer. You will be cared for by qualified mental health professionals twenty four hours per day. I understand from the State Department that Erie County Medical Centre is the most wide-ranging treatment psychiatric facility in New York State."

"My brother wanted me to see a psychiatrist but I thought it would obstruct my career. I thought *he* was the one who was nuts. He tends to be my watchdog. I never believed I had any problems, especially not that Post Traumatic Disorder thing." says A. J.

"Do you believe him now Officer Benson?" Dr. Kremer asks.

"You know, it's hard to comprehend. It seems so real. If my wife and son are not here, where are they?" he replies.

"Mr. Benson, arrangements have been made to fly you home in a few days on a private plane. You have been awarded much courtesy here because of the standing in your country. We understand from authorities in the states that at one time you even assisted in the repatriation of U. S. servicemen killed by the British in the war of 1812." Miss. Rushton says.

"Yes, that's true. Twenty nine Americans buried in what was then British soil. We dug them up, examined their bones and then took them back to the states for burial. It was a very rewarding and moving experience." A. J. says.

"Officer Benson, you will spend two more days with us until we can finalize the arrangements for your transfer. During that time you will undergo some psychiatric tests. In addition, you will continue to be treated for your bodily injuries." reports Dr. Kremer.

"I am grateful" says Benson "I truly am, and I am sorry for what has happened. I didn't mean for it to happen and wish I could take it all back" he says. "I feel bad for all of you and I feel bad for my friend Erin. All she wanted was a little friendship. She tried hard to help me find my family." he continues.

"Officer Benson" says Inspector Angus "Erin is dead. She jumped from the top of her building tonight. From all reports, she spent some time on the rooftop drinking lager and contemplating life. Then in a flash, she jumped onto the sidewalk below." Angus says.

"That too is my fault. I just want to leave here. Please allow me to go home." A.J. begs.

"You'll be leaving Edinburgh Turnhouse by private charter on Wednesday morning with a police escort. Until then the doctors here will work with you to regain some of the mobility in your arm. Your wounds are healing well, but they need a great deal of physiotherapy to get back to normal. You also need a great deal of psychotherapy." Dr. Kremer reports.

The meeting is over when Benson signs the documents presented by the Crown Attorney. Benson is escorted to a hospital room that he is unfamiliar with. It is not a locked police room but is a regular hospital room. He is offered regular bed clothes and afforded some of the other comforts other patients receive. A policeman remains posted outside the door. The deportation will take place on Wednesday morning.

Benson remains a guest of the Scottish people for now.

Chapter Twenty-six

Dave Alexander was not looking forward to the blood and guts meeting with his superiors from the Buffalo Police Department. His flight from Edinburgh was uneventful but filled with anticipation. Not even the in-flight movie provided a respite for the nervousness he felt about meeting his superiors. The only thing that relieved his feeling of doom was the reflection of the very friendly and beautiful constable that drove him to the airport as well as the inspiring view from the window of the 767. The view of the southern tip of Greenland from 35,000 feet was clear and magnificent. He wished he could land on one of the thousands of icebergs that had slid down the mountains and now bobbed in the frigid coastal waters.

His flight was on time, his connection on time and his arrival in Buffalo, exactly on time. "Thank you Continental Airlines for being so fucking on time." he thought to himself, thinking he would have loved to have been delayed for what he felt was the meeting to end his career. But, as reliable as ever, Continental Airlines pulled through and delivered Super Dave Alexander to the gate at Buffalo International Airport on time; and deported.

Dave wasted no time in retrieving his bag before heading to the passenger pick up area in the lower level. His anxiety was lifted somewhat when he heard the voice of Ken Stratten summoning him to his waiting car. Alexander was shocked when he realized that Leanne, the ball breaking Chief of Detectives was nowhere in sight.

"Ken, hey, you on your own tonight?" Dave asks with trepidation.

"Fortunately yes. Lucky prick you are for sure. Now get in Dave, we've got lots to talk about." replied Dr. Stratten, happy to see his friend.

The two men sat quietly through the parking lot fee paying booth and remained silent until out onto the busy I90 expressway.

"So what happened to the Chief?" Dave asks "I thought she'd be tagging along tonight.

"She's been pretty good through this actually Dave; she gave me full responsibility to pick you up, get you home and freshened up. You're not off the hook by any stretch of the imagination. There is a meeting planned with the Chief of Police and Chief Ronalds and members from your Association. The meeting is set for day after tomorrow. I guess then you'll get all the shit dumped on you. From what I hear Dave, they're not pissed at you going to Edinburgh to look for A. J. at all. What they're pissed at is the stink that the Edinburgh Inspector made about you misrepresenting the reason for your trip. Why did you even go to the police over there anyway?" said Ken.

"Courtesy I guess, and in case anyone was concerned about me and why I was asking questions about Angela's family. I didn't know it would blow up in my face so fucking fast over there. Your brother sure caused things to happen fast. What do you hear from him?" asked Dave.

"He's being deported from Great Britain on Wednesday." replied Ken.

Laughing he says "Deported is such a strong word isn't it? There's another thing I have in common with your brother, we've both been given the boot from Bonnie Scotland." he replied with a laugh.

"You guys were always tight, weren't you Soop?" a smiling Ken replied. "Now you're both fugitives from the fucking Queen!"

"So tell me about A. J. What's the story with him and the charges in Edinburgh?" Dave asks.

Ken Stratten maneuvers the car through the evening traffic and light snow toward Dave's home in North Buffalo.

Dave, unlike you, my brother is being escorted home on a private jet. He is deported from Great Britain, just like you. He's been given the private flight because of his illness. I should rephrase that about being given the flight. It cost me $35,000 for that flight back to Buffalo. After 9/11, no airline wants to fly crazy people, or people presumed crazy, especially those being deported for criminal acts. He has been given more treatment for his wounds over there and some initial psych evaluations. He's signed a contract that compels him to undergo full psych treatment at ECMC when he returns. If he refuses, he will be arrested immediately on federal charges and sent to trial. I put the deal together with the State Department and the Crown Attorney for Edinburgh." Ken reports.

"Money talks and bullshit flies home I guess."

Dr. Stratten pulls the car into the driveway of Dave's modest home and bids him good night. It's been a long couple of days for both men. Both are exhausted, both are worried about A. J. and both are unsure of what A. J.'s future might hold. But more than anything, they are both extraordinarily worried that there is much more about the disappearance of A. J.'s family yet to be uncovered.

"Doc, there is something big I need to talk to you about." says Dave.

"What is it Dave, you look like you've seen a ghost or something." Ken Replies.

"Doc, it didn't take long to determine that Angela and Jimmy are not in Scotland. I think even your brother knows that, which really makes me think about why he went there in the first place." Dave says.

"He's a sick man, very sick. You don't know how sick someone can get when they ignore their mental health issues. I've urged him and implored him to see the specialists in the field that I know. He just wouldn't admit he had a mental problem. He figured that once he got the 'all clear' after the shooting, he returned to work. The Erie County D. A. set the trial for Brent Carl in record time. A. J. was pressured by the D. A. to provide most of the evidence in the trial. The D. A. met with him for days and days, pressed him for those important little details, and maybe some that he did not recall immediately. A. J. was in a pressure cooker. The D. A. became very aggressive with A. J. in order to draw out more information about the test crash facility. He couldn't handle it. He was already suffering from post traumatic stress disorder at the earliest stages, but this pressure from the D. A.

only fertilized the onset of the PTSD.

"Yes, I remember those days for sure Ken, your brother was really put through the fucking ringer by that asshole D. A. I think he could smell the victory and was ready to bask in the limelight. At A. J.'s expense I might add." Dave says.

"That's for sure Dave. I remember thinking at one point in that trial, and I wasn't there every day, that the D. A. and the prosecution team were treating A. J. more aggressively than the defendants. Then he had the defense attorneys to content with." Ken says.

"They were a lot easier to digest than our own fucking D. A." Dave affirms.

"What do we do now Dave? I mean, while you're able to help. You're going to be put through the ringer on this one. Honestly I don't think they'll terminate you when they fully realize why you took that trip on your own time." Ken says.

"Doc, I am certain that Angela and Jimmy never left the States, or the City for that matter. It tears me up to say this, but I think that A. J. has done some harm to his wife and son. It's just too clean, the house with not a hair out of place. Poof! Just gone." Dave regretfully reports.

"But he jumped at the chance to take the lie detector and he passed the fucking thing too!" Ken says.

"Yes, he did at that. Doc, do you think that someone in his state of mind could fool the polygraph to the extent that the investigators wouldn't even consider him a suspect?" Dave asks.

"Dave, I am not an expert but I've read extensively on the syndrome since A. J. was shot and spoken with Dr. Liberte about this very phenomenon. From my understanding, someone who is guilty of a crime, and who committed this crime while in this type of depreciated mental state brought on by untreated PTSD, could in fact completely deceive the polygraph. The most incredible thing is that this person does not recognize himself as the perpetrator." Ken says.

"You mean that he may have done something to his family but doesn't know it? That's weird stuff. It's bloodcurdling when you think of the consequences."

Ken replies "Dave, we need to do a couple of things as soon as we can. We need to admit A. J. to ECMC Psych Services the minute he arrives back in Buffalo on Wednesday. I will have Dr. Marisa Liberte work with A. J. to see what she can get out of him. I'd do it, but he won't respond the correct way with me. Dr. Liberte is a well known Psychotherapist and Hypnotic Practitioner. She has more degrees behind her name than I can mention. She'll speak with him in a certain way and ask all of the questions in a well thought out order. In addition to the other psychotherapy she may hypnotize him in order to extract the most repressed feelings that A. J. has. Marisa's the best, and she's fully willing to work with us. Then what we need to do my friend is find out what happened to Angela and Jimmy."

"How do we do that? We have absolutely nothing to go on do we?" asks Dave

"No we don't but that's your department Dave, you're the cop." Ken says with a touch of humor "and once Dr. Liberte gives us anything, any little tidbit of information at all we'll investigate the hell out of it. The nice thing is that Dr. Liberte reports to me. She won't report to the Buffalo Police Department or the D.A. She reports to me and only me. I am A. J.'s Physician and by virtue of this, I am in complete control of any medical information about the man. It's a simple case of Physician/Patient confidentiality." Ken says.

"OK Doc, you know I'm with you one hundred percent. I just have to stay out of jail myself in order to help you." Dave says.

"Alright then, let's leave it at that. We've talked long enough tonight. You must be dog tired from your trip. Besides, my car is almost out of gas sitting here in your driveway" Ken says with a laugh.

"Like a couple of young lovers who can't say goodnight?" Dave replies.

"By the way Dave?" asks Ken "do you mind giving me back my Amex card now? I need to buy gas on the way home." He laughs.

Chapter Twenty-seven

The Challenger 605 is a sleek, newly built aircraft belonging to BAC-British Air Charter, a private jet operator out of Edinburgh's Turnhouse Airport. The small but mighty two-engined jet craft has a capacity of up to 12 people. It can operate at a maximum altitude of 41,000 feet, the same as the larger commercial jets. It takes the pilot only 22 minutes after take off rotation to climb to a cruise altitude of 37,000. It's a fast little jet with a beautiful trimmed spacious interior complete with bar, satellite television and full kitchen galley.

The 605 sprints her few passengers this day quickly across the Atlantic Ocean with ease. Traveling at 870 kilometers per hours, A. J. Benson can barely hear the humming of the two powerful Rockwell engines. Instead he chats with his two "associates" from Scotland Yard about their plans once they have off loaded him into the care of Buffalo Police. The two British Officers are looking forward to having a lively night out in Niagara Falls Canada after they land in Buffalo. It takes only 20 minutes from Buffalo International to reach the party city of Niagara Falls Canada, Las Vegas of the North. The officers plan to visit the new Casino Niagara, hit some of the local bars and of course, see the "Bloody Falls" and have some Canadian pints. A.J. gives them some pointers on the finer things to see on the Canadian side of the border. He tells them about the world famous "Seducteress Lounge" where the waitresses are more plentiful than the strippers. The fun at "Seducteress" carries on until the wee hours of the morning. "If you're really lucky boys" affirms A. J. "one of those crazy coked up waitresses will give you a hooter shooter!" The three men share a laugh. The two Scotland Yard escorts will have just about the right amount of time to spend being tourists until they turn around and head back to Edinburgh in the sleek Challenger.

A. J., when not acting like a tour guide, reflects on the happenings of the last several days. His clarity fades on the sequence in which the events took place. He wonders if he met Erin after he went to Falkirk; did he walk or take the train to Falkirk; who was the woman in the house on Wallace Street; how many pints in the pub; did his old friend Soop go to Scotland with him; how did he get to Scotland; he must have taken the train, I remember the trains; Waverley station is a busy place; all those people getting on and off trains, the long line of taxi cabs; Chester's; the diesel locomotives, watch out for the explosion!

He wakes briefly and rolls his head against the window of the Challenger. Then he drifts into a deep sleep staring out into the empty Atlantic skies. One of his escorts asks if he would like a pillow. There is no reply.

The large hand on the back of his neck begins to squeeze as his feet are lifted from the floor. He is elevated now, flying and spinning like an amusement park ride. He hits the floor hard, without lower his landing gear. Not again he thinks. He is a crash site on the floor of the tiny room. The hand of the monster reaches out again. His tiny arm is broken, blood trickles from his blackened nose and he closes his swollen eyes. The momentum of the attack slows, and then slows some more until it stops. The light through the hallway door ushers in the Angel. The Angel strokes him and cradles him before turning to face the sleeping monster. Noise comes from the mouth and nose of the monster whenever it breaths. The Angel moves close to the monster, caressing the noisy sleeping monster until there is no more noise.

"A. J., we're landing in Buffalo in 45 minutes. The captain wants us to use the lavatory, then strap in for the landing.", the escort requests while shaking the sleeping Benson.

A. J. wakes from his fog and nods in agreement. He remains seated for the remainder of the flight, saying nothing, appearing tormented.

HISTORICAL SOIL
PART TWO

Chapter Twenty-eight

The Comprehensive Psychiatric Emergency Program at Erie County Medical Centre is the only 24-hour psychiatric emergency program in Western New York State. The service offers evaluations in two stages. A registered nurse, social worker and a psychiatrist are part of the treatment team. Dr. Marisa Liberte leads one of the specialist teams dealing with Post Traumatic Disorders. Her unique approach using a combination of various treatment forms, including hypnotism achieves positive results. Her many successes in this area earned her the reputation of being one of the top psychoanalysts in the State.

Dr. Liberte uses hypnosis to recover repressed memories of sexual abuse or of past experiences. She uses hypnosis to discover truths hidden from ordinary consciousness by tapping into the unconscious mind where the truths allegedly reside. Dr. Liberte's long list of patients includes those who have been victims of or witnesses to a heinous crime. Police encourage them to undergo hypnosis to help them remember details from their experiences.

It is believed that hypnosis alters the brains electrical state, enabling the patient to recall events from their present or past life which they have conscious memory.

Dr. Liberte is anxious to meet her new patient and begin the RMT or repressed memory therapy. She is an associate of A. J. Benson's brother, Dr. Ken Stratten who has solicited her help. Dr. Ken Stratten has urged his brother to see a psychiatrist to address the ever increasing symptoms of PTSD. He has tried for over a year to make this happen for his brother but to no avail. A. J., the great almighty police inspector knew better. According to A. J., he was fine, and had fully recovered from the trauma of the shooting at the crash test facility. In actuality, he had healed physically from the gunshot wounds to his face. Mentally however, he was heading on a rapid downward slide directly into the face of his demons.

Dr. Liberte was surprised when she met A.J. in his quiet room in the Psych Department at ECMC. She was expecting to see a big, strong cop with lots of outgoing attitude and personality. Instead, she met a weak, trampled shadow of the man he once was. She was expecting to have to explain in detail and justify what her treatment plan would be. Instead, she received complete approval from A. J. for the treatment plan that will include a trip inside his brain by way of hypnosis. Here he is in front of her now this big strong cop now compacted into a small affable parcel of what he used to be.

"A. J., my name is Dr. Liberte, I'm a good friend of your brother." she says.

"Hello Doctor, my brother told me you agreed to help me." he replied.

"Yes I did agree, and the fact that you say it in that manner tells me you agree with him. About the help that is?" she asks.

"Doctor, I didn't put much stock into what my brother said in the past about my mental condition. In fact I thought it was a lot of bullshit. I had this really bad thing happen to me in Scotland. I had a nervous breakdown and hurt some people." He said.

"A. J., let me give you the first piece of advice of our relationship. I am the doctor, and if any definitions need to be attached to your condition, I will be the one to do it." she says firmly.

"What do you mean?" he replied.

"You are telling me that you had a nervous breakdown in Scotland when in fact you did not have a nervous breakdown. What you had is not described as that. You are suffering from Post Traumatic Stress Disorder. Period. No question about it. The fact that you have ignored your doctor's call for help only exacerbated the situation. You can ignore other symptoms that your body shows signs of, but you definitely cannot ignore what is happening in your brain. So, my friend, we will get to work on you to try to understand the best way to help you. There are a number of different procedures we can follow for treatment once we know what's in that little head of yours." she says with a half smile.

A. J. returns the smile gesture with one of his own. He appreciates her efforts to break the ice with him. For once in a long time, A. J. feels he is not in control of the situation. He is accustomed to being in control of every situation. After all, he is a cop, and a good cop at that.

"Mr. Benson I want you to know I am going to use a technique with you called hypnosis. Once I am confident you are in a relaxed state, and that your brain has accepted what we are doing, I will ask you a few questions. These questions are in no order and when I tell you what the questions were once you awaken, you may wonder what their significance is to your condition. I will only ask you ten questions or less. Your brain waves in this state of semi consciousness can not process more than a few questions. You will have no control over the answers. The answers will be honest and will hopefully draw out enough information so that I and the other members of the team here can suggest a treatment plan for you. Do you understand all that A. J.?" she asks.

"Yes Doctor I do." A. J. Replies.

"From now on, you will call me Marisa. I believe that by using first names it has an effect on comfort and the more comfortable you are with me, the more I can extract from that stuff between your ears." She says. "Understood? Can we proceed now?"

"Ready when you are Marisa" he says.

A. J. and Dr. Marisa Liberte make their way down through the brightly lit hallway without speaking to a small room near the end of the long corridor. They enter the room through a solid oak door. A. J. notices the door is padded with leather on the inside, presumably soundproofing the room. The room has subdued lighting, a leather loveseat, a leather reclining chair and a straight back chair beside a small round end table. A large circular Persian rug adorns the floor and adds a calming air to the place.

Dr. Liberte requests for A. J. to sit in the leather recliner chair to which he obliges. A. J. is in a rare relaxed state, considering the recent events and what has brought him to the Psychiatric Unit of ECMC.

"A. J., I want you to close your eyes and listen to the room for a few moments. Listen to all the little sounds in the room and concentrate on drowning those sounds out over the next few minutes. Do you understand?" she says.

"Completely." he responds.

Dr. Liberte adjusts the lights to a dimmer setting from her position in the high back chair. She watches her patient intently for signs that he is following the instructions. A. J. closes his eyes and intently listens to the sounds in the room. The padded door ensures that there no sounds are heard from the corridor or outside offices. She notices that A. J.'s eyebrows lift as he strains to listen to something, probably the air flowing through the room from the heating system. Over the next few minutes, she detects that her patient is in a state to embark on hypnosis.

Dr. Liberte gives no indication either by a clearing of her throat or other physical movement that she is about to ask a question of the resting Benson.

"Can you hear me?"

"Yes."

"Are you cold or warm?"

"Warm."

"Are you asleep or awake?"

"Asleep."

"Where are you?"

"In my room."

"What room?"

"My room at my mother's house, my bedroom. It's warm even though it is snowing outside."

"You sound nervous. Are you nervous or anxious about anything?"

"Yes."

"Tell me what makes you anxious A. J."

"I hear my father coming upstairs."

"Why does this make you anxious?"

"Because he will beat me up again, he hates me."

"Why does he hate you, do you know why?"

"No."

"Are you happy he is dead?"

"Yes, oh yes I am happy he is dead."

"Can you relax now that he is dead?"

"Yes, the angel protects me now that he is dead. The angel killed him for me. I am happy the angel put her wings over him and killed him. I am happy the ambulance took him away, I do not want to see him anymore, and mother and I are peaceful now. Thank you for killing the monster mother, thank you."

The questions end. Dr. Liberte does not want to overload her patient just yet, so lets him drift out of his visit to the past. The results are astounding so far. She writes in a steno pad as A. J. blinks and awakens.

"Very good A. J., you did very well." the doctor says, "Do you recall any of my questions?"

"Not at all, I was just listening to the room and that's all I heard." he states.

"Good then, enough for today, let's get you back to your room, lunch is served soon and you can rest this afternoon, watch a little television or read" the doctor says.

"May I go out for a walk?' A. J. asks.

"No, you may not, not yet. No one may visit you either I'm afraid. Perhaps in a few days we can give you those liberties, but not at the moment. I need you rested for our session tomorrow."

"I want to go outside, I need some fresh air. Take me outside Marisa, please. Can we just stand outside the door, I just need to get out, please." he begs.

"It is rare that a patient is granted this. Why do you want to go out so badly?" she asks.

"Honestly?"

"Of course, honestly, you can talk to me, what is it?"

"I want to get outside so I can run away from here. I want to go and see Angela and Jimmy." he says.

Shocked at what she is hearing, and amazed at the clarity and decisiveness of his statements Dr. Liberte decides to ask a few questions of A. J.

"So let's say I permit you to go and see them, do you need a ride to get there?" the doctor questions.

"No, I can walk, it's a nice walk."

"Where will you see them? Are they expecting you to visit them?"

"Yes, I normally visit them twice a week where they are. I bring Angela flowers. They are missing me and want me to come to visit them. I need to go to them." he states.

Maybe we can call them on the telephone and tell them why you can't come to see them." the doctor says.

"Maybe you can just fuck off and let me get out of here." he demands.

The doctor, sensing that a major crisis is developing in the room, raises the receiver on the intercom and dials a number. Immediately, two huge attendants enter the room and attempt to subdue a now frantic Benson. Benson is pacing the room back and forth like a caged and cornered animal.

"I need to see them now, let me out of here Goddamn it I need to go and see my family." He barks.

"Where are they A. J.? Where are they?"

"You are a cheating slut bitch." he shouts.

The attendants try to overtake A. J. but he is too strong. He knows too many moves from his years of physical police training. Even with a damaged left shoulder, he is still stronger and cagier than the guards sent to secure him. Dr. Liberte knows that something more sinister happening here. She has never had an adverse reaction to her hypnosis sessions and is perplexed. Trained in the procedure for years and practicing the procedure for decades she has never seen someone act like this. "Could he still be under?" she thought.

"A.J.!" she shouts, "Wake up!" she demands.

Another guard enters the small room and is punched in the face by Benson. The guard drops to the floor and is unconscious.

"Let me the fuck out of here." A. J. shouts at the top of his voice as he bolts toward the door, left open now by the last guard sent in to subdue Benson.

Not in any type of restraints at all, Benson is clear to run the corridor to the first fire exit he sees. He disappears down a fire exit and dives onto the panic bar on the outside door. Fresh air fills his lungs. His only thought is to see his wife and son. At top speed he runs toward an open field at the rear of the Medical Centre. He clears a fence by placing one hand on a fence post and thrusting himself over into the parking lot of an adjacent building. There, he catches a glimpse of a large man taking bottles to an outside recycling container.

At top speed and force, he knocks the man down to the asphalt with a body check, using the good side of his body. His injured shoulder is hurting, excruciating pain drifts throughout his body.

Benson leans over the man, still dazed from the collision with the cop, and tears his coat from his body. He pulls his good arm through the coat and tosses the collar over the back of his neck.

He hears the unmistakable sound of sirens, police sirens, closing in on his location. Without hesitation, Benson runs around the building and melts into the pedestrian activity of the bustling street.

Chapter Twenty-nine

Dr. Ken Stratten is between patients when he is informed of the morning's events by Marisa Liberte. He quickly mentions to his medical office staff that he will be leaving immediately. They will tell the waiting patients that Dr. Stratten was called to deliver a baby. Dr. Stratten has not delivered a baby since he was an intern at Columbia Presbyterian Hospital in New York. He rapidly dials the number for Dave Alexander, making arrangements for Dave to pick him up at his office.

In no time, Dave's Chev is waiting in front of Stratten's office.

"What the fuck happened Doc?" asks Dave.

"It's a nightmare for sure. I asked this renowned doctor to help me with my brother and he just about kills her. He's out of his mind and out of control." Ken says.

"Where is he now?" Dave asks.

"Let's head over toward Grider Street, behind the Medical Centre, maybe we can pick up his trail there." Ken says.

The two men sit, stunned and shocked, say nothing to each other as Dave speed toward Grider Street and the Expressway, a mere few blocks from ECMC. There, they notice a Niagara Frontier Transit Authority bus pulling into a stop to pick up the passengers waiting in the covered shelter. Out of the corner of his eye, Dave catches the sight of what seems to be a one armed man in a dark ski jacket.

"It's him, there Ken, at the bus shelter." he says

The NFTA bus pulls away from the curb and onto the Expressway. The two men follow the bus as it winds its way through its route. Ken and Dave wait behind the bus every time it makes a passenger stop to see if the one armed man exits. There is no way for the men to notify other police about their pursuit. Dave is officially off duty and does not feel he can involve police in this search. Both men are happy to remain on their own. The bus stops again after turning onto Delaware Avenue. No one exits. Strange the bus would stop and no one exit or enters the bus. The bus pulls away and within 25 feet, comes to an abrupt stop and discharges A. J. Benson from the rear doors.

"Let's just follow him from here, just for a minute and then we'll arrest him." Dave says.

"OK, sounds reasonable. Where the hell is he going?" Ken asks, "It looks like he's going into the cemetery."

The two men decide that now is the time they will approach A. J. so they speed up toward the iron gates of the cemetery only to be abruptly cut off my an approaching funeral procession. The funeral lead car with flashing purple light nudges between Dave's Chev and Benson, who they see now, is strolling casually into the cemetery.

Ken had only one thing on his mind as he and Alexander wait for the funeral procession to pass, so they can track A. J.

"Why is his brother visiting at Forest Lawn Cemetery?" Ken thought. Their parents are buried elsewhere, and Ken knows of no reason why A. J. would be visiting Forest Lawn.

Forest Lawn is a stunningly beautiful historic cemetery, consisting of 269 acres of rolling hills and valleys in the heart of the City of Buffalo. Entering through the main gates, Ken is aware of how striking the cemetery is. As they drive through the grounds on the winding roads, he is aware of the history of the place. Many old monuments dot the landscape, marking the final resting places of famous Buffalonians including Millard Filmore, Buffalo's entry as President of the United States.

"Where in hell can he be Dave?" he asks.

"This place is so fucking huge; I don't know where to begin to look. Do you want me to call for some back up, some extra eyes Doc?"

"Not just yet Dave, I want to find out why he's here first, why this place?"

"Over there Doc" pointing to a figure standing alone. "Is that him?"

"Can't tell, go around the pond here, come up from the other side and we'll get a better look."

"Yep, think that's him." Dave said.

"Stop here Dave, let's see what he's up to." Ken says.

Dave and Ken leave the car at the side of the narrow road and crouch behind the huge monument of Willis H. Carrier. He is the man who designed the first scientific air conditioning system and was later the founding head of the Carrier Corporation. The tall granite monument allows the perfect vantage point to observe A. J.

"What the fuck is he doing?"

"I can't tell Doc. Wait, what's that?"

A. J. stands stoically at the foot end of a grave marked by a relatively small black granite monument. Smaller than most in this section of the cemetery, it bears the name of *Anderson.*

A. J. opens the flap of his coat and reaches cross chest into a vest pocket.

"Shit Dave, he's going to kill himself!"

"No hold on Doc." Dave says as he holds Ken back behind the Carrier monument with one arm. "I've seen this before. He did the same thing at Waverley Station, that's how he got shot in the shoulder."

Slowly and methodically A. J. withdraws his right hand from the pocket and is now holding, tightly in his right hand, an assortment of what appear to be flowers.

"What the fuck, I don't get it." says Dave, looking questioningly at Ken. "Must be the grave of a friend or something. Why would he bring flowers here?"

With his right hand clearly visible now, holding flowers, he leans and places the bouquet on the grave, while at the same time, removing what appear to be old flowers from the same spot near the headstone. A. J. discards the wilted flowers off to the side of the grave he is standing on. After a few minutes there, A. J. lifts his right hand to his head and begins to cross himself.

"You guys Catholic"? Dave asks Ken.

"No, we're not. Our parents and A. J.'s father was Presbyterian. The only Catholics in the family were Angela and Jimmy."

"Why the hell would your brother cross himself?" replied Dave.

"You know better than anyone Dave that my brother is a sick man. You've been through hell for him. I am very afraid his disease is progressing rapidly. I have no idea why he is here."

Ken and Dave continue to observe A. J. as he walks slowly from the grave, glancing over his injured sling held shoulder as he walks down the slight incline to the road.

"Let's follow him Doc."

"Ya, right, but I want to see that monument up close first."

"Good idea, you check out the stone, I'll follow A.J. Looks like he's not in a hurry, so try to catch up" Dave says hurriedly.

Ken approached the grave where A. J. was standing with great trepidation. Not knowing why he was there, placing flowers and making like a catholic is confusing his brother.

The family name "Anderson" appears on the monument in large letters. Underneath the surname, and in smaller script are the names of Leroy 1925-1999 and "his beloved wife" Kathleen 1928-2002. "Gone to be with the Lord" is inscribed at the bottom of the monument. The monument seems to be very ordinary and does not set off any alarm bells to Ken. "Here lies a couple who were in their late 70's when they died" he reflects. "So why in the hell would my brother be placing flowers here and paying tribute to them?"

"Come on Doc!" Dave orders Ken as he pulls the car up along side. "Get in, he's changed direction and is just about at the main gates."

A. J. has picked up his pace as he heads toward the main gates of the cemetery facing Delaware Avenue. He is oblivious to the two men trailing him, giving Ken and Dave a chance to move closer to A. J. with the car.

"There he is, get up along side now. Let me out!" orders Ken.

Dave moves the Chevy around the section of the cemetery just inside the Delaware Avenue gates. He positions the car across the entrance in an effort to stop A. J. from leaving. "Unless he crawls under the car or jumps the fence, he's mine" Dave barks to Ken.

A. J., still unaware of what is happening notices the car across the entrance. Seeing his brother now exit the passenger side, A. J. stalls, stopping dead in his tracks. His mouth opens in amazement, a sideways glance and his arms extend as if to begin to run. Ken approaches his brother.

"Where in the hell have you been? You were to remain at ECMC on orders from God right down to me! What the fuck do you think you're playing at A. J.? How did you get here? Why are you at this goddamn cemetery, for Christ sake? What's with the flowers? Why are you crossing yourself like a mick? What the fuck is with you?" a frustrated Ken pebbles his brother with questions.

A. J. remains in a state of shock, unable to answer. The look on his face tells Ken he is in distress. His eyes begin to flutter as his body trembles. The shudder intensifies. "Something is about to give here", Ken tells himself.

"Talk to me, goddamn it, talk to me!" as Ken makes a move to grab the lapels of A. J.'s overcoat.

At the moment his hands connect with his coat, A. J. drops to the ground in a heap, his eyes rolled back in his head, vital signs absent.

"911 Dave, now!" the doctor orders.

The doctor rips open his brother's coat and shirt and begins to administer CPR. Not responding, Ken feels panic, but continues the CPR and mouth to mouth resuscitation.

Dave Alexander draws his cell phone like a revolver to call emergency services. The dilemma is advising emergency services where in the cemetery they are, how to give direction to the ambulance. Furthermore, trying to make it clear that he wanted emergency response to a cemetery was a bit out of the ordinary.

Ken was oblivious to the squeal of the arriving ambulance and was not aware that Dave had moved the car out of the entrance way to allow the paramedics in.

The paramedics paddle A. J. in an effort to restart his heart. Injections of adrenaline are slammed into his heart followed by more CPR. A. J. is bundled and lifted onto the waiting stretcher, continuing to show no sign of heart movement.

Ken jumps in to occupy a jump seat at the back of the ambulance after A. J. is loaded. The heart and respiratory monitor continues to beep.

"Come on A. J., come on." Ken says.

Suddenly, without notice, the monitor reacts wildly.

"OK, we got something here." a paramedic reports to all on board.

"I think his sternum is fractured." states another paramedic.

"Oxygen now, stop CPR."

"OK, he's breathing."

"They'll treat the fracture at the Centre." Ken interjects "I probably caused that when I initiated CPR."

"It's OK Doc, it happens."

He lends a hand to guide the stretcher carrying his brother into the emergency room entrance from the now idling ambulance.

"Hurry everyone, Room 3 Blue" an ER nurse announces to the arriving party. "Stat!"

The door to Cardiac 3 opens into a maze of medical machinery, monitors and tubes. A. J. is placed onto the table while more nurses and doctors arrive. More injections are administered while monitors are on strategic positions on Benson's body. The stick-on electrodes are wired to a waiting monitor. The hearts electrical impulses are traced onto graph paper emanating from the main monitor. A cardiac catheter is inserted through the carotid artery. The catheter is a menacing looking tool about 125 cm long and is designed to pass into the heart through a major vessel. It allows the determinations of blood pressure and the rate of blood flow in the vessels and chambers of the heart, and identifies any abnormalities. Medications are instilled directly through the catheter into the coronary vessels.

"Can I talk to you Doc?" Dave says as he opens the door of Cardiac 3.

"Do you need me?" Ken asks of the trauma team leader.

"No, we're OK, things are looking better Doctor" comes a response from a nurse.

Ken moves toward the saloon style door of Cardiac 3, looking back over his shoulder a number of times, as if waiting for someone to call him back for help. Outside the door waits his somber looking friend.

"Doc, I checked in the cemetery office about that plot out there before I left."

"And?"

"It seems the last burial in that plot was on August 16, 2002, the old lady Kathleen Anderson. That's nothing out of the ordinary. She was old, has a daughter who lives in the city, couple of grandkids, pretty normal shit."

"Is there any solid connection to my brother there?"

"Nothing obvious, but get this. The cemetery superintendent recalls speaking with your brother on several occasions over the last few months while he was visiting at that grave. He told me he puts flowers out there all the time. In fact, he had a complaint from the old lady's family about it. It seems every time they came to visit the old lady at the cemetery, there were already flowers on the grave. They wondered who was placing them there."

"I don't get it Dave, can you make anything out of that."

Hesitating while drawing a deep breath, Dave announces "It's the date Doc."

"What fucking date?" Stratten nervously replies.

"The old lady was buried on Friday, August 16, 2002. She died on Wednesday August 14th."

"Yes, OK, she died and she was buried, what's the connection to my brother?"

"The date Doc, August 15th, 2002, two years ago last summer. Ring any bells?"

"Holy shit. Angela."

"You think?" he stops short.

"August the 15th is the day A. J. went home to an empty house, I remember that date distinctly now. Not even the dog was there when he got home."

"Doctor Stratten, can you come back in here please, we need you." orders a nurse from the trauma room.

Chapter Thirty

Dave Alexander drove quickly as he left ECMC for the meeting with funeral director Harry Ridgeway. The Ridgeway Funeral Home is located North Buffalo, not far from where A. J. lives. Not only did Ridgeway Funeral Home handle the funeral arrangements for Kathleen Anderson in 2002, but they also provided one of the hearses for the repatriation of American soldiers from Canada years before. Harry and A. J. met when both men were members of a committee raising funds for the local Boys and Girls Club. Harry was on the committee to boost the profile of his funeral home business while A. J. held the position to boost him up the police department ladder.

Dave entered the funeral home by the rear door marked "Flowers." On the outside of the door a terse warning that flowers would only be accepted during certain hours.

Ridgeway appeared immediately. He is a short man, a little over 5 feet tall with a ruddy complexion. He has an obvious bad hair transplant that appears not to have aged as the rest of his hair had. It is rumored that the hair transplanted to his head is his own pubic hair. Just about everyone in the community knew that while Ridgeway seemed outwardly compassionate and caring, he was a true narcissist with what people call the 'short man syndrome'. Harry would tell anyone who would listen about purchases of new vehicles, new clothes or renovations to his business or home. Ridgeway never ventured too far away from Buffalo for holidays or weekends. He felt he was the only one competent of serving the families of the community the way he did. He allowed his wife to raise their three lovely daughters by default. He could never keep staff because he never let them perform the duties they were hired to do without a lot of criticism or interference.

Ridgeway had a reputation within the funeral profession as being a poor embalmer and a bragger. He is a Mason and Master of the local Masonic Lodge. No matter how many secret handshakes he gives as a member of the Craft, or how many Grand Lodge meetings he presides over, he is essentially a cheating dog of a person who wouldn't hesitate to carry on an affair with his best friend's wife.

Even at his height and aging appearance, he had the local reputation of being a ladies man. He had been accused on several occasions of bedding down the office girls he had working for him. On these occasions, Ridgeway had wined and dined them at the country club and dazzled them with his affluence. He is the epitome of narcissism. He would make use of his funeral home and guest house for sex with his female staff. On one such occasion, his best friend and husband of his female embalmer surprised the two of them in a downstairs lounge, sitting in the dark, obviously post playtime. Fifteen minutes earlier and he would have caught them in the throws of passion.

One such affair resulted in the pregnancy of this female embalmer. She gave birth to a son and hoped that Ridgeway would leave his family for her. He did not. After being told about this affair and birth of a son, Ridgeway's wife immediately ordered the termination of the female employee. As this fact became better known in the community, his business decreased and the popularity he enjoyed in the past soon waned. His long time marriage soon showed strains, a result of his years of unfaithfulness. Not wanting the public humiliation of a divorce, the two lived apart and would intermittently be seen out for dinner in local restaurants as if to tell the community that everything was fine in the marriage. It is generally known in the community that Ridgeway was living in his funeral home, while his wife and daughters stayed in their lovely suburban home.

A. J. knew this of Harry, but the two men got along quite well. A.

J. helped out around the funeral home, doing body removals, driving the hearse or setting up flowers whenever Ridgeway called for some help because of his pissed off employees quit without notice.

"I need any information about that Anderson family I called you about on the way over. Any subtle details you have might help my investigation." asked Alexander.

"Not much to tell from what I remember of them. I buried the wife a couple of years after the husband passed away. Put them both in the family plot at Forest Lawn. Good solid oak caskets and a lined burial vault."

"What's a burial vault Harry? Not sure I know," said Dave.

"A burial vault is an outer box made of reinforced concrete. Some are lined with materials to make them water resistant. Its sale increases the cost of the funeral nicely too. I make as much on that as I do some caskets. The casket is lowered into the vault and the lid is sealed on. We used to call them grave liners or rough boxes in the old days." Ridgeway adds.

"Do you take this vault out to the cemetery yourself?"

"No", said Ridgeway "the vault company delivers the vault to the cemetery first thing in the morning on the day of the funeral. They drop it in the open hole and wait for us to arrive. The lid alone weighs about a thousand pounds." he replies.

"When is the hole dug?" Dave asks, uncomfortable referring to the grave as a hole.

"Cemeteries normally dig the graves late afternoon before the funeral, especially if there are several funerals the next day."

"So, you arrive at the cemetery on the funeral day with the hearse, casket and all. The casket is placed on the grave, and then lowered into the vault. This correct?"

"Exactly."

"So let me ask you this. Doesn't an open hole pose a danger in the cemetery if dug the day before the funeral?"

"Not really, the grave is covered with plywood to prevent anyone from falling in the open grave. It's never been a problem because the cemetery digs the grave so late in the afternoon the previous day, there is not usually many visitors." replied Ridgeway.

"So who knows the hole is dug ahead of time?"

Ridgeway contemplates why this question is being asked.

"Obviously the cemetery people know, because they do the digging. The only other people that know these details are me and my staff. Why?

"Holy shit." Dave says aloud as he leaves Ridgeway's funeral home.

Chapter Thirty-one

In the few minutes it took Dr. Stratten to discuss matters with Dave Alexander outside of the ER, the trauma team performed their magic and stabilized A. J. He remains connected with tubes and electrodes, reminiscent of the Frankenstein movies of the 1930's. Ken feels relief that his brother is stabilized but is also experiencing a great deal of nervous tension as a result of what Dave Alexander had reported and intimated about burial dates in Forest Lawn Cemetery. Nothing seemed to make sense. His brother was his first concern, not his only concern, but his first concern so he turned his energy to the emergency at hand.

In a matter of 45 minutes after being stabilized, A. J. was wheeled to the ICU suite for continuous monitoring of his heart muscle and other vital functions. Ken reflects on how technology has extended the lives of people who have suffered debilitating heart attacks, and that no technology exists to cure what ails the mind. Ken sits vigilantly at the bedside of his brother, praying that he recovers and praying that some truth is finally revealed about the disappearance of Angela and Jimmy.

Chapter Thirty-two

Dave Alexander waits outside the door of the meeting room where his disciplinary hearing had been held earlier. The members of the Board, representatives of the Police Association, and the D.A. for Erie County had interrogated Dave for over three hours about his involvement in the Edinburgh fiasco. Dave has resolved himself to the fact that his simple misstatement to the Lothian and Borders Police could in fact cost him his job on the Buffalo Police Department. The committee asked Dave about three hundred questions in three hours, all of which he had a reply for. Whether or not it was the replies they wanted to hear is another issue, but regardless, he is waiting outside the door of the hearing room, his career hanging by a thread.

"Officer Alexander, you may return to the hearing room." a voice says from behind the door.

Dave enters the hearing room and takes his seat in front of the presiding panel. He tries to read them but cannot. "They don't look too pissed" he thinks to himself. Dave's mind is really on his friend A. J. and situation at the hospital. Dave is pleased with himself that he was able to uncover what little information he did from the Cemetery Manager and from Harry Ridgeway. His feelings are all over he place; the disciplinary hearing, the missing persons case, and of course his buddy Benson.

"Officer Alexander, after reviewing the testimony you have given to this panel regarding the Edinburgh situation, the committee is now in a position to render its opinion." Chief Leanne Ronalds announces.

Dave wants to say "Well, that's what we're here for so let's get it over with."

"Officer Alexander, this committee has taken considerable time to judge the answers you have given in response to our many questions. The decision that we are about to render is by no means unanimous, in fact quite a lengthy discussion occurred as we reviewed your answers. We want to be fair to you Officer Alexander, you have been an employee of the Buffalo Police Department for many years. All members of the panel deliberated intently about the disciplinary charges against you. We are sorry that it has taken us so long to reach some sort of decision."

Dave can feel himself sinking into the hard oak chair even though he wasn't. He can feel an itch in his feet and rejects the idea to bend over and stick his finger into his sweaty shoe. "Come on you fuckers" he thinks to himself, "get this over with." The tension mounts as the Chief, representing the entire committee is ready their decision.

"The misstatement to the Scottish Police is regrettable and has caused a great deal of consternation on both sides of the Atlantic and in the offices of the Crown Attorney in Scotland and the District Attorneys Office here at home. However we, the committee, looked at the incident in its entirety, meaning that we reviewed exactly what led up to your visit to Edinburgh in the first place. We examined the evidence you gave about the incident in Waverley Train Station. Officer Alexander, there is one conclusion and one conclusion only." Said Ronalds. "Do you wish to hear the verdict of this committee at this time?

"Yes Chief Ronalds I would." replied Alexander, with feet itching and hands sweating.

"Would you stand please." requested the Chief.

"Officer David S. Alexander, regarding the disciplinary charges brought against you, namely misrepresenting your position to an outside police department, we find you not guilty." Said the Chief.

"Holy fuck." Dave replied aloud, then catching the inappropriate statement he said "I am very sorry for that, thank you for finding me not guilty." Dave continued.

"Officer Alexander" continues Ronalds, "While we find that fact that you lied to Inspector Scott Angus in Edinburgh is objectionable, we also realize that this was the only way to help our brother Officer A. J. Benson. You not only gave of your own holidays and expense to travel to Scotland to first of all find Officer Benson, but to attempt to return him to the states without incident. Unfortunately, his episode in the Waverley Station was no fault of yours, it would have happened sooner than later, whether you had connected with him over there or not."

The Erie County Assistant District Attorney pushes his chair back and stands beside Chief Ronalds.

"Officer Alexander, I want to thank you, on behalf the Erie County DA's office, for your devotion to your job and to your brother officer. These actions will not be soon forgotten as you are to be commended for the actions you took, not only here but in Edinburgh as well." Says the ADA.

"Thank you Officer Alexander, you are free to go. You are expected to return to work on your next scheduled shift." concludes the Chief.

Chapter Thirty-three

Sodium Amytal is a hypnotic sedative drug that, like hypnosis, is occasionally used with trauma survivors to access repressed or unconscious material. The sodium Amytal and hypnosis is used by only trained practitioners who avoid leading questions. The appearance of Dr. Michael Bricks from McMaster University in Hamilton, Ontario is a welcome sight by Dr. Marisa Liberte. Dr. Liberte has summoned the leading expert on sodium Amytal to Buffalo to investigate whether this medication should be administered to A. J. Benson, in an effort to determine the fate of his wife and child.

Dr. Liberte has had several emails and phone calls from other practitioners from throughout the state and her own hospital voicing their objection to the use of what they perceive to be a primitive drug and primitive procedure.

Dr. Ken Stratten is one of the doctors who do not feel that sodium Amytal is the best decision.

"Dr. Stratten," says Dr. Bricks "The drug sodium Amytal is from the same family as the drum Nembutal, Seconal and Pentothal. These medications are quite common don't you agree?" ask the doctor.

"Yes they are, but wasn't Amytal used during World War II, the Korean and Viet Nam Wars as a truth serum for captured spies?" asks Ken.

"Yes it was, and there is current debate that any form of torture administered by armed forces around the world should be halted at once and replaced with the Amytal Interview. It is much more effective and less invasive. The prisoner or spy, still believing he is withholding the truth, is actually telling all he knows to the enemy. No harm comes to the prisoner, it is quite humane compared other forms of torture that have been used in the past." Dr. Bricks says.

"How can we be sure that what A. J. is saying is actually what happened? After all he did participate in the polygraph test when this investigation was newly opened?" ask Ken.

"Yes, that's true" adds Dr. Liberte "but the way that this medication is administered causes the patient to be drowsy and slurred of speech, but most importantly awake."

"Dr. Stratten, we will administer small amounts of the drug, by vein, every few minutes. This procedure usually takes about an hour. Your brother will be awake but in what we call a twilight state. We employ this procedure to examine the unconscious. The dominant theory is that people under Amytal could not possibly lie. This is why it receives the designation of truth serum." Dr. Bricks adds.

"My brother has just recovered from a heart attack. Although he has been doing well over the past several weeks, I am concerned that the sodium Amytal might irritate something and cause another infarct or stroke." Ken says.

"That's very unlikely Dr. Stratten. Amytal is not that type of drug. The way in which the Amytal is administered, by IV drip, is another guarantee that we will not have another occurrence. If we notice anything out of the ordinary, we can immediately stop the drip. We abide by the published treatment guidelines of the International Society for the Study of Dissociation.

Dr. Stratten struggles with what he has heard from the experts Dr. Bricks and Dr. Liberte. The decision weighs heavy on his mind, but none the less he reaches a conclusion.

"Doctors, I would like to assist you to prep my brother for the Sodium Amytal Interview as soon as you possibly can." concludes Stratten.

Chapter Thirty-four

A. J. rested comfortably in the leather reclining chair in the room at Erie County Medical Centre he escaped from several weeks ago. He cooperates fully with the Amytal interview.

"Ken, Dr. Bricks, Dr. Liberte, I want to help you so please ask me anything. I want to find out where my family is more than anything." A. J. says to the room full of doctors.

The drip is prepared and A. J.'s arm is swabbed with alcohol in preparation for the needle. That accomplished, A. J. drifts off into a dreamlike state, but remains awake.

"A. J. this is Dr. Bricks. I am going to ask you one question and one question only, is that alright?"

"Yes, of course." he replies

"A. J., your brother tells me that you went home one day a few years ago and discovered your family was missing. Can you tell me what happened that day when you got home?" he asks.

"Angela was quite happy to accompany me and Jimmy that afternoon. I had asked the two to join me to take a look at something I was planning to do. The invitation was well received. We had not been out as a family together in a long time. When I arrived home that day, Angela, Jimmy and Maggie the Mut jumped into the car. I was feeling very good this day. Unencumbered with thoughts of work I was a free man for now to enjoy a rare outing with my family.

Jimmy's wanted to stop at McDonalds for a drink and something to eat so I stopped the car and ran into the restaurant. I purchased a kids meal with fries and a soft ice cream for Jimmy. I bought a Big Mac and fries for Angela and I bought Maggie the Mut some ice cream.

I went to the washroom before going back to the car and put a good dose of Angela's sleeping medication into the ice cream that I knew Jimmy and the dog would eat first.

When I drove into Forest Lawn Cemetery I received questions from Angela and Jimmy.

"What's this place dad?" Jimmy asked

"A cemetery son, you know what it is." I replied

"Why are we in the cemetery A. J.?" Angela asked.

I ignored the questions for now, only wanting to drive to our final destination. I drove slowly around the beautiful monuments and gardens until I reached a place where recent excavation has resulted in a hole in the ground.The dog was the first out of the car, and ran around the area where I parked the car. The dog pissed on every square inch of ground. Maggie the Mut, with her red collar and silver dog tag license clinking was the first to feel the effects of the narcotic.

Angela asked me what are we doing here, and I told her that I wanted her to see an open grave. My friend Harry Ridgeway told me that they were getting a grave ready at Forest Lawn to bury old Mrs. Anderson the next day.

A. J. went on to describe his conversation with his family.

"Are you fucking nuts A. J?" Angela barks.

"No, I just want you to see what an open grave looks like, OK?" he replies.

"A. J. get us the fuck out of here right now! This is crazy talk. I am sick of all the open grave shit you spew. You're so turned on by bodies and open graves it makes me sick and afraid. Get us home." Angela says.

"It's not a scary thing at all, or crazy. It's someone's final resting place." he says. "Just come and look how dark and beautiful the earth is six feet down in the grave." he says.

Angela took Jimmy by the hand and moved to where I was looking down into the hole. She stood with me for a while trying to understand my motivation to look in this empty grave.

"Just look at the earth, it's so fine. Looking into an open grave in a cemetery like this is like looking into history. Do you know how many famous people are buried here?" he asks. "Can you see Fillmore?"

"A. J. you are fucked, what the hell you are talking about, can I see Millard Fillmore? You're starting to scare me and I want to go." she demanded.

Angela looked over at Jimmy who by now was sitting by himself on a bench near a gravestone and has fallen asleep. The dog too is sleeping at the foot of his young master. She becomes terrified.

"Home now A. J.! I mean it, now!"

A. J. turned to his wife. "You fucking slut."

"What the hell is that about?" she asked.

"You know fucking well what it's about. It's about you in the back of a van, getting fucked by cops." He said

"How do you know about that?" Angela replied.

"For fuck sake darling, I'm a cop. That's what I do. I find out what scum shit like you are doing and confront them with it."

A. J. added "Angela was dumbfounded. She moved toward Jimmy but I grabbed her arm and stopped her. I jerked her hard toward me while I continued my sermon on the evils of fucking my co-workers. Angela, for once in her life, has no reply, no lie to tell, no bullshit to spew. There was no opportunity for her to speak, especially as the butt of my Glock revolver is battered into her scalp. She melted to the ground as if a wicked witch hit with water. She hit the ground in front of me and without a bit of hesitation I kicked her drunken cheating ass into the open grave.

She moaned.

I returned to my car and opened the trunk to retrieve a pillow. I brought the pillow to where Jimmy and the dog were sleeping and placed the pillow over his Jimmy's face. The angel's wing. I applied just the right amount of pressure to suffocate his little body, and then I picked him up and deposited him in the open grave with Angela.

Drs. Bricks, Liberte and Stratten are speechless until Dr. Bricks asks of the others "Is this enough?"

Stratten returned the answer "No, we need to hear it all."

"The dog is asleep, really feeling the effects of the doping. I placed the same little pillow over the snout of the dog and throttled the life out of it. I hated that fucking dog. I then threw the dog in with the rest of the family."

Sleep tight; don't let the bed bugs bite. If they do, hit them with your shoe and they won't come back another night."

"I could see the chipmunks, ducks and swans throughout the cemetery. So much life to enjoy in a place reserved for death."

"I took out a shovel from the trunk of the car and jumped down into the open grave with Angela, Jimmy and the dog. I put about two feet of the dark rich historical soil on top of them. I laid them side by side in the open grave and then shoveled dirt from the mound left by cemetery workers who dug the grave for the morning burial.

I padded down the earth around them so they could not be seen when the concrete vault is delivered the next morning. I scaled back up the side of the open grave to see the setting sun. I replaced the three inch piece of plywood that covered the grave after the workers dug it. I crossed myself when I got out of the grave. I don't know why because I'm not religious. Then I threw the pillow and the shovel in a wooded area on the way back to my car."

The details of A. J.'s interview were bone chilling. Many of the questions about the disappearance of A. J.'s family are now answered, but many more prevail.

The interview is over, the drip is withdrawn from his vein, and A. J. sits quietly facing his brother and the other doctors who are trying to compose themselves. Dr. Bricks has conducted hundreds of Amytal interviews in the past several years but this one has clearly shocked and dismayed him. The look of utter exhaustion is on the faces of Dr. Bricks and Liberte as A. J. reenters the real world. Dr. Stratten sits in the corner of the small room in tears, overcome by the shear trauma of learning that your dear brother has murdered his own family.

"What is it Ken?" asks A. J.

Dr. Bricks avails himself of this opportunity to discuss the effects and side effects of the Amytal drip.

"A. J., you have been administered a chemical drip that results in you telling us the truth. We have asked you about the disappearance of your wife and son. Do you understand that?"

"Yes, of course. I want to learn about what happened to them more than anyone. What happened to them?" A. J. requests.

The three doctors look at each other as if the other is prepared to speak. All three are still in a state of total disbelief about what they have just heard from their patient. Can this be truthful? Can this actually have happened or has the patient short-circuited the procedure and has just explained a dream? Was A.J.'s description the true nightmare experienced by this family or was the description simply a hallucination as a result of the drip?

"A. J., when you were under the influence of the Amytal, you became very relaxed, more relaxed than anyone I have ever tested" said Dr. Bricks. "You told us in a well organized style, and in chronological order how you came home one day a few years ago and asked your family to join you for a little outing. Do you remember telling us this fact?" asks Dr. Bricks.

"No, I don't remember talking about that." he replied.

"Do you remember telling us that you took your family to McDonalds that day and while you were there you poisoned the food that was purchased for your family?" Dr. Liberte asks.

"That is ridiculous, I can't recall saying that." A. J. replies.

"You obviously don't recall providing this information to us at all do you A. J.?" asks his brother.

"Why do you go to a grave in Forest Lawn Cemetery A. J.?' asks Dr. Bricks "and why do you bring flowers to that grave and cross yourself like a Catholic would do?

"What is your attraction to open graves?" asks Liberte.

"Why did you go to Scotland to look for the family that you already killed and buried in that grave at Forest Lawn?" asks Bricks.

A. J. Benson is peppered with questions from his doctors that pertain to his concentration to a strange grave at Forest Lawn Cemetery. The more questions solicited, the more unnerved Benson seems to be.

In an effort to not to demoralize Benson any more and in fear of a repeat of the last escape from the psychiatric ward, the doctors decide to end the discussions and allow the Buffalo Police Department discover what the truth really is.

Chapter Thirty-five

A meeting to discover the facts about the Benson case was convened at Buffalo Police Headquarters and chaired by Chief of Detectives Leanne Ronalds. Also in attendance is Inspector Dave Alexander, the Messer brothers and Pathologist Selina Doodeman.

The meeting agenda was basically about what we should do, how we should do it and when should we do it. The first chore at hand was obviously to discover more about the burial of the Anderson family in Forest Lawn, because this was the grave that A. J. has been placing the flowers on and crossing himself when he leaves it. Detective Lex Messer was dispatched to meet with the Anderson family and deliver them the news that an exhumation order will be commenced. Dave Alexander suggests that another meeting with the womanizing funeral director Harry Ridgeway is in order and agrees to meet with him as soon as possible. He would like to ascertain what A. J. really knew about the open grave being prepared in advance of need for the burial of Mrs. Anderson. He wants to know if Ridgeway had any knowledge of what Benson might have been planning.

Detective Jake Messer will organize the physical dig at the cemetery with the management of Forest Lawn. An exhumation order must be issued by the local District Attorney and County Coroner. Ay time an existing grave is disturbed for exhumation, the Medical Officer of Health must also provide a certificate of exhumation basically stating that there were no plagues or epidemics at the time the burial took place.

The physical dig is easily arranged. The cemetery management will coordinate the necessary equipment and manpower to dig the grave and remove the burial vault containing the body of Mrs.

Anderson. The vault company contracted by funeral director Harry Ridgeway will be summoned to Forest Lawn to hoist the sealed concrete vault out of the grave. Once lifted from open grave, the burial vault will be positioned on a flat bed truck and removed to one of the cemetery garages. This procedure is done in an effort to provide privacy and keep the odor of the rotting decomposing body of Mrs. Molly inside the vault away from those working in the vicinity of the grave.

Dr. Selina Allison prepared her forensic team to retrieve the bodies of Angela and Jimmy Benson and Maggie the Mutt for forensic investigations which would include x-ray, autopsy and toxicological tests based on the information provided by Benson about the poisoned food given to his family and the dog.

The meeting is concluded and the parties at hand are dispatched to perform their respective chores. The early morning exhumation and is planned for exactly one week.

Chapter Thirty-six

While his friend A. J. Benson seemed to get along quite well with funeral director Harry Ridgeway, Dave Alexander clearly did not like him. He, like many others in the community, felt he was a bit of an egomaniac, especially for his short stature. Alexander is not impressed with Ridgeways reputation as a cheating slough of a husband either. Even though Dave has never been married, he still believes in the sanctity of marriage and believes that if and when he ever took his marriage vows, they would be adhered to for the rest of his life.

Alexander drove directly to Ridgeway Funeral Home from his meeting at BPD headquarters. He entered the rear flower door of the funeral home as he had done before. This time he was not met by Ridgeway as expected. Dave wandered around the spacious facility but saw no one. There were no funerals being conducted at the time and no visitation wakes being held. The place was dark. Alexander, confident no one occupied the main floor of the funeral home decided to try the lower level and proceeded over to where a sign indicated 'lounge and washrooms'. Dave descended the stairs and advanced through a short dark hallway until he heard rustling.

Dave entered the 'lounge' where the rusting was more audible. Dave moved around a corner in the room and was not totally surprised to find Harry Ridgeway and a cute little thing sitting side by side on the couch, sipping what looked like tea. They straightened up considerably when he entered the room, the woman standing, pulling her skirt back down into place and then exiting to what appeared to be a staff washroom.

"Hey Dave, nice to see you, what's up?" said Ridgeway.

"If you can manage to straighten yourself out Harry, I have some things I need to speak with you about" Dave asks.

"Sure, just be a minute here Dave." says Ridgeway as he organizes himself.

Ridgeway immediately joined Dave who has taken a seat behind a small desk in the hallway of the lower level of the funeral home.

"Harry, for Christ sake, I'm not talking to you with that bulge in your pants." Dave says with disgust. "Dipping your quill in the company ink again Harry?" he adds.

"What is it?" Harry demands in a more serious tone.

"I spoke with you before about the burial of a woman in Forest Lawn by the name of Kathleen Anderson. Do you remember?" asks Alexander.

"Yes, something about a burial in Forest Lawn wasn't it? So what do you want to know now?" he asks.

"Harry, our friend A. J. Benson has revealed to investigators that he may be responsible for the death of his wife and son."

A gasp from Ridgeway.

"Furthermore, he has indicated that he put their bodies into an open grave. We followed A. J. to Forest Lawn several weeks ago to the grave of Kathleen Anderson, the woman you buried on August 16th two years ago. We believe that A. J. killed Angela, the boy and the dog and put them in that grave the evening prior to the burial. Harry, did you notice anything when you arrived with the funeral procession the day of Kathleen Anderson's service?" asks Dave.

"Dave, when we get to the cemetery after a funeral, the burial vault is already in the ground, so how the fuck would I see anything?" he replied.

"Well Harry, I don't know, I'm just asking alright. Is the plywood still covering the grave when you arrive with a funeral?"

"No, the vault is in the ground as I said, then the artificial grass is placed around the entire area and a lowering device is placed over the open grave. When we place the casket on the lowering device, you can't even see into the grave most of the time. If you did, you'd only see the inside of the concrete vault. When the preacher is done praying, we hit a little toggle that lowers the casket slowly into the vault. So, no I didn't see anything and wouldn't expect to" said Ridgeway. "Not this day or any other."

"Harry, did A. J. ask you when the next burial would be there, or at any cemetery?" Dave asked.

"Not specifically on that occasion, but he did asked regularly when we had funerals because he often helped out if he was off that day." replied Harry.

"So he never specifically asked if you were having a funeral on that day, that particular day August 16th?"

"Not specifically no. But one thing does kind of stand out in my mind about things with A. J. around that time and that was his obsession with decomposing bodies, and skeletons and that funeral he was on at Fort Erie. He would always question me about how quick a body would decompose in the ground." Harry said.

"So what would you tell him about that?"

"Well, the only thing I knew for sure and what I told A. J. was that a body decomposed at different speeds due to the type of earth they are buried in, the temperature of the ground and how long the body has been in the ground. If the body is in a sealed up vault, the decomposition is slower because the body is not in contact with the earth directly. Fuck I had no way of knowing he was asking for a specific reason." Harry added.

"OK Harry, thanks for your time. Sorry about the shot earlier about the girl. I was out of line." said Dave.

"Don't mention it Dave. It's been an ongoing thing for a while for me you know. I had a hot little bleached blonde embalmer working here a while back. She was married and I knocked her up. I was happy with the great blow jobs and afternoon delights, but she wanted more. Dollar signs you know. Her husband was *nice* enough to call my wife and tell her about it. He was a Brother Mason, I never thought he'd rat me out. Since then Dave, I've been living in the funeral home here apart from my family." Harry said.

"Even Masonic dogs get their day Harry." laughs Dave as he exits into the cold Buffalo air.

Chapter Thirty-seven

Normally Forest Lawn Cemetery is a quiet place this early in the morning. There is a buzz in the air this day as the exhumation is about to begin. Today is the day that the concrete vaults containing the remains of Kathleen Anderson are being removed from her grave. Investigators from the Buffalo Police Department want to explore whether this grave was intended to be the final resting place for Angela and Jimmy Benson.

The commotion in Section 17 this day is reminiscent to that of a movie set. All the actors are in place, the props are heated up and ready and the cameras are ready to roll.

The large yellow backhoe lumbers up the slight incline into the section from a yard in the distance toward the back of the cemetery property. Unlike the normal bucket of a construction backhoe, the narrow bucket on this machine ensures an exact dig within the confines of the grave. Vehicles carrying police officers, the Medical Office of Health and cemetery workers arrive in unison. The occupants of these vehicles exit and stand around the grave of Kathleen Anderson and look down onto the snow covered grave as if they could see something already. The cemetery foreman asks for the appropriate paper work from the Medical Officer of Heath. Cemetery workers plot out the dimensions of the grave as the narrow bucket backhoe moves into place over the grave.

One well placed scoop after the other, the earth is lifted high above the onlooker's and deposited into a dump truck. Once this operation is concluded, the same earth will be replaced over top of the burial vault containing Mrs. Anderson.

Chief Leanne Ronald arrives as the tractor lowers its boom and moves away from the opened grave. The burial vault, with gold paint and nameplate still visible is surprisingly not that far underground as most of the onlookers had assumed it would be. Cemetery workers are shocked that the vault is so high in the ground. The normal depth of a grave is about six feet. When a burial vault is placed to accommodate a casket, the distance between the surface and the top of the vault is reduced, but never this much. Dave Alexander leans over to Dr. Stratten and tells him that he suspects the vault is higher than normal because something is buried underneath the vault.

Cemetery workers jump down into the open grave with spade shovel to remove the earth from the top and around the burial vault to make its removal that much easier. The ground is hard and chunky but not frozen solid. Burial takes place all year round in this area because of the mechanical means by which the graves are dug.

The foreman summons over a truck from The Buffalo Vault Company, providers of the concrete burial vault. The boom from their truck lowers a heavy metal cable into the grave. Workers standing on top of the vault in the grave attach the cable to the same metal hoops used to lower the vault into place two years before.

Once the large metal cable is attached to the hoops and secured, the foreman gives the sign for the vault truck to raise the consignment from the depths and onto its own flat bed.

As soon as the vault is clear of the grave, the boom swings the entire device in the air and onto the truck. The truck is then directed away from the excavation site.

All eyes are focused inside the grave. Dr. Stratten, anxious to know if his brother really did kill his family and deposit them into this grave is the first to look down into the empty hole. Dave Alexander joins him immediately, as does Chief Leanne Ronalds. Dr. Selina Allison with her forensics crew joins the others at the top of the grave. Cemetery workers and the manager of Forest Lawn Cemetery also gather around the empty grave. Dave Alexander happened to look up and see everyone staring down into the hole and wondered if that many people were at the funeral in the first place? It is very evident to everyone that there are no other bodies in this grave.

All participants of the morning exercise were expecting to view the rotting corpses of A. J.'s family and pet dog under the massive vault. This did not happen. There is no sound other than that of the diesel engine of the departing truck from Buffalo Vault.

"There! Right there look!" yells Dr. Stratten.

He points to a small ridge of earth at the north end of the narrow grave.

"There! There! There!" he screams.

The cemetery foreman is the first to jump down into the open grave with a spade. He is joined in an instant by Dave Alexander with a spade of his own, snatched from the hands of an on looking cemetery worker obviously too afraid to jump into the hole. Dave follows the direction by Dr. Stratten as he motions where to plunge the spade deeper into the ground. Dave thrusts the blade of the shovel at exactly the place indicated by Ken Stratten. He pushes the blade deeper into the soil with his foot and pulls down heavy on the shovels oak handle.

"The dog!" says Chief Ronalds loud enough for all to hear as if narrating.

In one lift that required several grunts by Dave Alexander, he lifted the drippy not yet skeletonized remains of Maggie the Mutt. Collar and dog tag intact he held the dog in the cradle of the shovel while the onlookers gasp. A very small bag, resembling a body bag is tossed down into the grave by Dr. Allison. The foreman opens the bag while Ken unceremoniously drops the remains of the dog into it.

Chief Ronalds clears her voice and announces "Alright, I want you two men out of the grave now. This is now a crime scene." She says.

She motions to one of the uniformed officers to secure the area and place yellow crime scene tape around the area. Everyone is asked to step back as the officers fence the area off with the tape that has "crime scene" printed on it.

The cemetery foreman and Dave Alexander repel up the side of the grave and are given a hand onto the solid ground by Ken Stratten and the horrified public servant from the Health Department.

"Thank you for your help sir but if you're going to puke please leave the cemetery" says Chief Ronalds to the MOH.

The pouch containing the body of the little dog is placed into the trunk of a police car by Dave Alexander. Dr. Allison removes a cell phone from her bag and calls for body removal, presumptuous of more bodies being located in the open grave.

"Alright, here's how this is going to work from here on in. The only personnel I want around this grave until otherwise notified are members of the Police Department and Erie County Medical Examiners Office. Got that right everyone?" Alexander asks.

"Yes, good move Dave." says Dr. Stratten.

"Doc, did you hear your name mentioned there? I want you completely away from the crime scene. Seeing your nephew and your sister in law in this state is not something you will easily forget, so for that reason, you are requested to join the others." Dave says firmly.

The cemetery and vault workers have retreated to the small operations office near the large frozen pond near Section 17. Dr. Stratten unhappily joins them.

The work inside the open grave following the departure of the civilian workers was done quickly and professionally. The two men assisting Selina Allison were directed by her to begin a scoop and sift at the bottom of the grave. A scoop and sift is a method used by archaeologists when excavating ancient graves in order not to disturb any valuable evidence.

The workers scoop and sift for about five minutes until a small shovel catches some silk like material in the grave. Further scooping and digging with a trowel reveal that the material is from the soccer shorts worn by Jimmy Benson. Jimmy's remains appeared to lie more on their side than flat. Perhaps this is due to the weight of the vault crushing the bones of the family as they lay dead in a grave that is not really theirs. More scooping and digging reveals the decomposed body of the little boy. The body is not fully decomposed. The skin has become leathery and black. Soil remains visible in the young boy's mouth. His legs and arms are grossly distorted. Ribs begin to show through the chest cavity. Already, grim evidence is being unearthed about the brutality of the murder.

Dr. Allison assists in lifting what is left of Jimmy Benson out from beneath his earthen grave. Doing so has exposed what appears to be a portion of the collapsed head belonging to Angela Benson. Brain matter had seeped out of the cranial cavity doe to the weight of the concrete vault. His body moreover, does not lay flat in the ground but rather sideways with a pointed hip digging into the earth and his right shoulder slightly elevated.

Jimmy's body is placed into a full sized vinyl pouch and zippered shut. It is then raised to the ground by attendances using ropes in the six plastic handles that surround the bag. The movement of the earth in order to remove the dog and Jimmy has finally caused an odor to appear. The cold Buffalo air has aided in keeping the odor at a minimum, the rancid stench of rotting flesh now becomes evident.

The examination and removal of the full size body of Angela Benson will prove to be more complex and painstaking.

Dr. Allison is already aware of something of a phenomenon, something peculiar in each of the three bodies. She notes that for bodies that have been in the ground for about two years there is not the extent of decomposition that would normally be present. This puzzles her as she prepares to scoop and sift the body of Angela Benson.

The first order of business for the forensic team in the grave is to uncover the body as completely as possible in order to determine mode of death and positioning of the body at the time of death. Allison suspects that if what Benson says in his Amytal interview is true, that he may have taken some time to position the bodies in the grave. Uncovering the body in the correct chronology may reveal evidence to possibly suggest a motive for the murders and possibly indicate the participation of others in the death.

The earth is moved caringly from the top of the body of Angela Benson. Her completely clothed body is now in full view. Photos are taken; measurements using miniature rulers are taken and then photographed. Soil samples from the earth that circumscribed the three bodies are taken, placed in plastic jars, sealed and labeled. Sampling of the soil may reveal why preservation has been so evident in these bodies.

Dr. Allison moves the skull of the middle aged woman to one side to identify any marks or indentations on the skull that may have caused death. The air inside the grave is now steamy with the small of rotting flesh and decomposing bodies. The odor and is drifting to the surface, a fact noted by Dave Alexander who also adorns a face mask over his nose and mouth.

Also noted by Dr. Allison are two palm sized pieces of what appear to be plastic material in the grave that would have been centered on the chest of the female decedent. At closer examination, Dr. Allison realizes that this material is actually the silicone pouches that were the breast implants of Angela Benson. "Not so perky now are they?" Dr. Allison says to her rotting client.

In his initial report to Dr. Allison, Alexander reported that A. J. said he hit his wife on the back of her head with the butt of his gun. Dr. Allison reveals damage to the skull to substantiate this fact.

Hoping not to find the same scenario with Angela's body as she did with Jimmy, Dr. Allison reviews the angle in the positioning of her body. She notes that like Jimmy, Angela seems to be leaning to one side, her one shoulder lower than the other pointing into the earth. Dr. Allison is struggling to learn why this is the case with both bodies.

Moving the head of the woman to the opposite side reveals that she too has a mouthful of earth. Her nasal passage is full of soil. Dr. Allison is alarmed, for she knows what this might be indicative of.

The shear weight of the concrete burial vault caused the bodies to be compacted somewhat and pushed further into the soft earth, made pliable by cemetery workers digging the grave to bury Mrs. Anderson.

The body of Angela Benson is fully uncovered now and ready for removal from the borrowed grave. A zippered body pouch is dropped into the grave. Dr. Allison is hoisted up from the sepulcher leaving her assistant there alone temporarily while waiting for assistance to pouch the body.

Dr. Allison removes her gown, rubber gloves, face mask and shoe covers and moves quickly over to her vehicle. A steno paid is retrieved from a binder. Dr. Allison makes notes on a pad at a feverish pace, documenting on paper the thoughts she had while scooping, sifting and examining the bodies in the grave. She has been presented with a number of challenges during her dig as to why the bodies are preserved so well, why each had one shoulder lower in the ground than the other and why there is so much earth in the mouths and nasal passages of both of the bodies.

Angela's body is hoisted from the grave and is placed beside that of the dog and her son in the back of the Erie County Medical Examiners van. As instructed by Dr. Allison, the coroners van leaves the cemetery to deliver the human and animal cargo to the morgue. The autopsies are scheduled for mid day. In a matter of hours, the causes of death will be known.

The diesel truck from Buffalo Vault Company re-emerges from the garage holding area to redeposit the body of Kathleen Anderson into her rightful final resting place.

"Just one moment!" yells Dr. Allison.

She directs the operator of the vault truck to lift the vault from its platform. He obliges which allows her to scrape the bottom of the vault for any evidence. After all, the vault rested on top of these bodies for two years. Scraping the bottom of the concrete vault may reveal some evidence to unlock the secrets of the burials.

The sequestered Dr. Stratten, cemetery manager and workers and the Medical Officer of Health now return to the grave as the uniformed police remove the yellow tape that adorns the trees and bushes around it. The boom operator is given the "all clear" by the cemetery foreman to replace the vault into the grave. This is done expediently as is the refilling of the hole with soil, removed earlier to expose the bodies. The frozen sod is replaced over the disturbed earth and patted down by the workers to give the grave the appearance that nothing has been disturbed.

"Rest eternal grant unto Her oh Lord, and let light perpetual shine upon Her"

A light mid morning snow falls as Dave Alexander and Chief Ronalds lead the procession of police vehicles away from the grave in Section 17.

Chapter Thirty-eight

Considering that her hypnosis treatment of A. J. Benson was unsuccessful, Dr. Liberte is grateful for the effort and participation of her Canadian counterpart. In administering the Amytal drip, Dr. Bricks fruitfully extracted the information from Benson's head that had been so elusive for the past two years.

Dr. Marisa Liberte is a strong willed, energetic person normally. When she enters a room, it fills with her dominance and energy. But not on this day. As she walks down the hall of the locked psychiatric ward at ECMC on her way to meet with her patient she is somewhat reserved, her step much slower than normal and her energy worn out. She's been this way since Benson's Amytal interview. Through her decades of psychiatric practice, she has never been witness to such a horrific and atrocious act. Initially she believed that the Amytal, so called truth serum, would not be effective and secretly believed it was something from a spy movie. Her faith in the Amytal interview is unyielding now as she anticipates how she will deliver the results of the interview to Benson.

This is the concluding interview with Benson. He will be charged with two counts of murder following this meeting. The Messer brothers wait for the doctor outside the room that holds A. J. a prisoner now. When she is finished with Benson, they will be the officers to charge him, hand and leg cuff him and remove him to County Jail.

"Good morning gentlemen." says the Dr. to the officers.

"You too Doctor." they reply in unison.

Dr. Liberte breaks a slight smile when she hears the Messer Brothers greeting in harmony. Their reputation is well known and they are well liked.

"Lets get on with it shall we gentlemen?" she asks.

Dr. Liberte punches the keypad with a code and the three enter the room holding Benson. He looks pale and withdrawn. An untouched plate of breakfast food rests on a table beside the bed. Benson is without greeting this day, withdrawn and into himself. Liberte can only imagine what his reaction will be to the news she is about to deliver.

"A. J. I'm here to talk to you about the results of the Amytal interview that you took last week. Do you understand?" she asks.

"Yes, I understand, what would you like to talk about Dr. Liberte?" he asks.

"A. J., when you were under the influence of the Amytal drip, you discussed the disappearance of your wife and son. You essentially solved the puzzle for us, do you know that?" asks Dr. Liberte.

"I recall talking but I'm not clear what I talked about." he said.

"A. J. you are not supposed to be clear on what you talked about. They call Amytal truth serum. Did you know that?"

"Not really, I think I heard it being used in the war or something, to catch spy's right?" he said.

"Yes, but the clinical uses are much more refined these days. Essentially you told us what happened to your family" she said.

"I did? How did I know? So are you going to tell me where they are?' A. J. asked.

"A. J. we were all very shocked when you told us that you murdered your wife, your son and the dog and dumped them into an open grave" Dr. Liberte said.

"What the fuck?" he asked. "That's completely crazy."

"A. J., during the interview you told us about picking your family up and taking them to a grave that you knew had been opened at Forest Lawn Cemetery. You apparently knew this information by accident, from your funeral director friend. He must have mentioned it when you asked him if he had any funerals on the calendar."

A. J. sits, listening to Dr. Liberte, but does not understand how he knew about the murders.

"A. J., you told us that you picked the family up and took them for a drive, stopping at McDonalds for some food, food that you put poison in to feed your son and the dog. You had bigger plans for your wife."

"Bigger plans?" he asked.

"Instead of doping her, you asked her to come to look into an open grave, at which time you hit her on the back of the head with your service weapon. Do you remember telling us this information at all A. J." she asks.

"Certainly not, I am confused, you mean they are dead? I thought they were in Scotland. I went there you know, to Scotland to look for them. Wasn't that nice of me to go and look for them?" he said.

"A. J. you told us about striking Angela on the back of the head and pushing her into the grave. You then picked your son up, who had by this time gone unconscious with the drugged ice cream, and put him in the grave with his mother. Then you did the same to the dog. You went on to tell us that you covered them up with enough earth to hide them from view." She said.

"I don't recall talking to you about that, I think you're making this up." he said.

"A. J., yesterday morning a team of forensics experts and police inspectors uncovered the grave where you placed your family. They removed the burial that was interred on top and uncovered your wife and son, with the dog, underneath a concrete vault. Dr. Allison noted that the back of Angela's head had been hit with a blunt instrument. She noted the positioning of the bodies and it is the same positioning you described during the Amytal interview." She said before being interrupted by Lex Messer.

"A. J., I have known you for many years, you were a good cop and it hurts me to do this." said Lex.

"Do what buddy?" A.J. replied.

"Andrew James Benson, I am placing you under arrest for the murders of Angela Benson and Jimmy Benson. The charge is two counts of first degree murder. Please stand up, put your hands together behind your back A. J." he orders as his rights are read aloud.

Lex Messer places handcuffs on Benson's wrists while Jake Messer places leg cuffs on his ankles. A. J. obliges and is the perfect prisoner. He does not protest at what is happening to him. He is clearly insane. The shadow of the former cop is walked calmly out to the waiting BPD van, where he is secured in by another cuff attached to the floor boards of the van.

Dr. Marisa Liberte is clearly upset, more upset than she has ever been after working with mental patients of all descriptions. As Lex and Jake Messer drive away from Erie County Medical Centre psychiatric unit, Liberte is weeping openly, sobbing uncontrollably.

Chapter Thirty-nine

The autopsy suite at the Erie County Medical Examiners office is bustling with activity. The body of Angela Benson rests on Autopsy A, while Autopsy B holds the body of Jimmy Benson, with Maggie the Mutt at opposite end of the table as if at the feet of his master.

The scene is solemn as the first cuts are made into their bodies. Dr. Allison conducts the post mortem examination on Angela while her assistant Dr. Dawn Ryan begins to cut into Jimmy. The tables numbered A and B are side by side stainless steel tables with a gutter running around their perimeters. The foot end of the table connects directly into large stainless steel sinks. Large dissecting knives that would make O. J. Simpson proud hang on a wall over the sink. This suite is furnished with high speed floor fans that operate virtually silent sucking the vulgar and offensive odors down from the noses of the technicians and doctors and into ductwork that spews out the stench on the roof of the building.

High tech voice activated tape recorders are installed over each of the autopsy tables. Directional lighting, the same that appears in hospital surgical operating rooms, light the way for the doctors and technicians probing the now rotting bodies of the Benson family. No matter how high tech or well lit and ventilated, the autopsy suite is a place where bodies are dissected and dismantled in an effort to determine their cause of death.

This is the same autopsy suite that a few years before contained the bodies of FBI agent Grant Norman and Mr. el Hakim following the disaster at the Buffalo Research and Innovation Centre. Table A was used for the autopsy of Brent Carl's son following the fiery crash of his Lexus on the I90.

Work has begun on the thoracic region of both bodies. The technician uses a scalpel to make incisions from both shoulder areas to just below the breast bone, then on a line to directly over the pubic bone. The large knives are used to separate the tissues and cut through the layers of tissue and fat to finally expose the internal organs.

This being completed fairly expeditiously, Dr. Allison and Ryan concentrate on the head and cranial areas of both bodies.

They simultaneously cut the scalps from ear to ear, deep enough to expose the shiny skulls of mother and son. A wedge is used to separate the scalp from the skull, pushing the scalp forward to cause it to extend over the eyes and face. A Stryker saw is plugged in to cut the skulls from one side to the other at two difference levels. A tap with a surgical hammer causes the skull to detach, exposing the milky looking road map that is a human skull. Small blue and red vessels run throughout the mass. The technician used his hand to detach the silky tissues around the brain from the side of the skull. In his right hand he hold a surgical knife that he directs into the base of the skull to sever the brain from the spinal cord. With both hands cradled, he places the entire brain on what resembles a kitchen cutting board.

Dr. Allison examines the damage to the tissue on the back of Angela's head and determines that she was indeed hit with a blunt object. The damage to the inner tissue of the scalp do not show the signs that the trauma was that intense. Certainly it was enough to perhaps disable someone and make them lose consciousness, but the blow on the back of her head did not kill Angela.

Dr. Ryan noticed no trauma on the body of Jimmy Benson at all. So how did he die?

Dr. Allison requests the assistance of Dr. Ryan to examine Angela's head wound closer.

The two doctors speak low as they lean head to head over the body of Angela Benson. There is a sober discussion between the two pathologists before Dr. Ryan returns to the body of Jimmy Benson.

In unison and with the help of their respective technician, they center their investigation now on the mouth, throat and lungs of the bodies. The thoracic cavity of the bodies remains intact, meaning they have not been eviscerated yet. This enables both doctors to see into the bodies and identify anything that may have caused their death.

Dr. Ryan is the first to raise her hand to the overhead dictating recorder, pulling it closer to her mouth as she examines the throat and lungs of the young boy.

Dr. Ryan speaks conclusively as the technician removes the tongue, trachea and lungs of the young boy. Her concise reporting as these body parts are placed on the cutting board that straddles the table draws the attention of Dr. Allison. Assisted by her technician she is approaching the same anatomical area of investigation on Angela. A few minutes pass as both doctors hold the lungs of their wards in their hands. Both doctors are rapidly dictating results of their investigations into the machine. Blood and body fluids run down the gutter of the autopsy tables from the dissection of the lungs and airways.

Dr. Ryan completes her examination of the airways and lungs first, due mainly to the reduced size of the specimen she is working on. Dr. Allison takes another half hour or so to come to her conclusion. Both doctors direct their technicians to complete the evisceration of the bodies and do the appropriate recording. This done, the technicians will place the viscera in a plastic bag and drop it back inside the open thoracic cavity.

Dr's Allison and Ryan are anxious to speak with Chief of Detectives Leanne Ronald, and hastily make the call from the wall phone in the autopsy room. The call is made in such alacrity that Dr. Allison dials the phone without removing her latex gloves that are still dripping with body fluids, fatty tissue and blood.

Chapter Forty

Once showered and dressed in street clothes, Dr. Allison is quite a stunning woman. She arrives at the offices of the Buffalo Police Department for her meeting with Chief Ronalds. Ronalds greets her at the entryway to the detective division and the two make their way to the Chief's private office.

"I hope you don't mind that I invited Ken Stratten here for this meeting?" asks the Chief.

"Of course not, poor guy, he needs to be here to listen to my report. It won't make him feel any better I assure you, but nonetheless, he has been an intricate part of this investigation from the onset. I'm pleased you invited him and sorry that I neglected to call him earlier." said Dr. Allison.

The two enter the office where Dr. Stratten and Dave Alexander are seated.

The professional formalities aside now, the air is cleared to hear the results of the post mortem examinations on the bodies of Angela and Jimmy Benson.

Dr. Allison clears her throat and begins to speak.

"It is hard to believe that the results I am about to speak of have been perpetrated by a member of the Buffalo Police Department. It would be hard to believe that anyone could cause these results, not just a police officer. In my opinion I believe that A. J. Benson knew exactly what he was doing when he killed his family. He knew that by bludgeoning Angela on the back of the head that it would likely cause her death. He knew that by including a high concentration of sleeping drug in ice cream that it would likely kill his son and his dog. Benson was a cop for a long time, but for a longer time he has had emotional and mental problems that are only now coming to light." Dr. Allison says.

"So tell us something we don't know." asks Dave Alexander.

"Yes" says Dr. Stratten "Can we please hear what caused the death of these people?"

"Of course you can, that's why I'm here. I want to warn you that the cause of death is not anything you bargained for." Dr. Allison continues.

The Chief interjects "Can we please agree no press on this, I'm fearful now of a backlash when this news of the autopsy results get out. If the cause of death is as bad as Dr. Allison is eluding to."

"Can we please get on with this, please?" asks Ken Stratten, outwardly uneasy at what he is about to hear about this brother killed his wife and son.

Dr. Allison continues "During the dig, we noticed several things that required red flags for follow up. The first thing was the amount of soil in the mouth and airways of both bodies. The second item was how the bodies seemed to be slanted as they lay in the grave, slightly downward on one shoulder. We couldn't figure this out right away, but feel that now we have looked inside the bodies, we know what has happened."

Dave Alexander stands and begins to pace the floor, looking nervous at what he is about to hear.

"We now know that death was not instantaneous. The blow to the head did not kill Lucy, nor did the fall into the open grave. The medication in the ice cream did in fact kill the dog, but did not kill Jimmy, nor did the fall into the open grave kill Jimmy." the doctor reports.

"So what did kill them doc?" asks Stratten.

"Hold on to your seats here everyone. When A. J. kicked Angela into the grave, she was not dead. She was unconscious, but not dead. When he threw his son into the grave, he was not dead, he was unconscious. Simply put, Angela and Jimmy survived the night in the open grave. They had enough air to breath but both were in an unconscious state. The stupor only lasted for several hours and this is when we know that both Angela and Jimmy became somewhat active in the grave. I mean that they stirred slightly in the grave enough for them both to move onto their sides to gasp for air. This is why their bodies were on a slight angle, because they were actually in a state of convulsion at this point." Said the pathologist.

"So they just ran out of breath?" asked the Chief.

"No, absolutely not. While they weren't breathing well, they were breathing. Let's say if they were rescued from the grave at about this time, there is an excellent chance they would have survived. They both inhaled a lot of soil and dirt, that's what we saw in their mouth, throat and lungs. This is what tells me they were alive in the grave for quite some time. When they did begin to move, it was not enough movement to cause them to be uncovered." She says.

"So help me understand what caused their death?" asked Ken Stratten.

"Ken, what caused their death was the weight of the burial vault being dropped on their bodies as they lay there twisting in the grave. They were buried deep enough by A. J. not to be noticed by the cemetery workers or the guys from Buffalo Vault Company. They were killed by the weight of the vault. When the concrete burial vault was lowered on top of them it crushed them, killing them at that moment. The dog was the only immediate fatality, killed by the ingestion of the poisoned ice cream."

"Well, that about wraps it up doesn't it, how sad and how shocking." said Dr. Stratten.

"Not so quick" replied Dave Alexander. "We know through the efforts of Dr. Allison and her team that A. J. did in fact cause the death of his wife and son. He had no idea that they were still alive when he shoveled earth in on top of them to cover them up in the bottom of the grave."

"We red flagged a couple of other things last week at the dig that I would like to reveal to you now." Dr. Allison says, as she defers to Dave Alexander.

"When I stepped on the spade to dig the dog out of the grave, I heard a clinking sound. When I brought the dog to the surface, I looked at what was left of the animal to see what might have caused the clink. There was the nice metal and rope collar complete with name plate and dog tags from the City. On closer examination, I noticed finger prints on the collar and on the name tag of the dog. There were no prints distinguishable on the dog tag, but there was on the little plate of metal that said Maggie the Mutt. I removed the metal collar and name plate and had the prints lifted and run through by our lab." Dave said.

"A. J.'s prints?" asks Ken.

"No Ken, not A. J.'s prints at all. They were yours!" replied Dave Alexander. "Your prints were on the collar and back of the name tag, large enough to be distinguished and lifted for comparisons. I retrieved your fingerprints from your State Medical Licensing application."

"Are you nuts Dave, what are you saying" Ken says as he lifts off his chair.

"Down sir!" order the chief.

"Well, I couldn't figure that out either right away. It wasn't until I ran the history on your American Express Card that things started to fall into place." He said.

"What the fuck Dave, what is this shit?" Ken shouts.

"Down sir, don't let me warn you again." said Chief Ronalds.

"When I ran the history of the card I got a stack of hotel and restaurant receipts back. To check this out is elementary, but time consuming so I solicited the help of Officer Emery Walter and the Messer Brothers to help me. We investigated and spoke with a lot of people who work in the hotels, restaurants and bars that you and Angela have been frequenting. Ken you have been a regular sexual companion of your sister in law for quite some time. There exists a great deal of evidence to that effect, so please don't try to debate it." Dave says.

"I didn't kill these people." said Ken.

"No, not really."

"What the fuck do you mean, not really? I didn't kill them even if Angela and I were seeing each other." Ken replied.

"No you didn't kill them, but you positioned your brother to kill them."

"Why would I do that?" Ken asks.

"For the oldest reason there is Ken. Angela was about to reveal your affair to one and all. It seems she grew tired of fucking cops all over town and wanted to settle down with a doctor. Yes, a doctor, even if it was her brother in law."

"This is nuts, I'm leaving." announced Ken.

"No you are not leaving Ken." continued Dave "You capitalized on your brother's refusal to treat his Post Traumatic Stress Disorder and manipulated him into killing his family. When I was researching your licensing with the State Board, I also uncovered the fact that you had taken courses at University in what was then a new treatment at that time. A new treatment called hypnosis. Ken we know that you hypnotized your brother regularly in an effort to drive him crazy enough to chase his family all the way to Scotland."

"And I did this how, detective Alexander?" Ken asks.

"Simply, you hypnotized him whenever you had the opportunity, but your hypnosis methods were flawed. I had to ask myself why Dr. Liberte had so much trouble administering her hypnosis treatment when she has done it successfully hundreds of times. With the help of Dr. Liberte and Dr. Bricks, we administered another Amytal interview to A. J. this week after the bodies were uncovered. Under the influence of the Amytal, A. J. told us that you had hypnotized him a number of times in the past year or so. Your technique and skills were inadequate and poor, the hypnotism it didn't really take hold." Reported Dave.

"Bullshit! My brother heard the tape about the time and temperature and finally got it in his head to go to Scotland to look for Angela.

"Not exactly Ken. You see, while I was in Scotland I solicited the help of a pretty constable by the name of Janet Angus. She investigated who might broadcast the local time and temperature on a telephone tape. She investigated all of the telephone and satellite systems in that country and came up empty. I was perplexed by the fact that this type of broadcast is non existent in Scotland. It was you Ken, you who planted that information on your brother's phone and in your brother's mind. You invented it, you delivered it and then you waited for him to act on it. But, he didn't act on it right away did he? He waited for months and months until he went to Scotland. It wasn't until after you tried hypnotism on him one more time. It was then and only then, he got it in his head to go to Scotland. The fact that you had also hypnotized him into being an alcoholic only added to his madness." Dave concluded. "And you chastised him as his doctor about his drinking and eating habits."

"We further discovered that on one of your starry-eyed romantic outings with Angela, she brought her little dog along for the ride. Seemed she wanted to be a tiny family with you. While you and Angela drove home from the Buffalo Chop House one evening, the little dog sat between the two of you. You stroked his neck and ears while you drove, leaving your fingerprints all over the little tag and metal part of the collar." Dave reports.

"How did you know we were there?" asked a deflated Ken Stratten.

"Not only was your credit card used there when you and I dined, but it was used when you and Angela met there before heading off to the Holiday Inn for a night of fun. I couldn't figure out why our waitress knew exactly what kind of wine to bring you the night we ate at the Buffalo Chop House. When I asked our little waitress friend Jodie about it last week, she remembered serving you and Angela the same wine. According to her, Angela really loved the wine, made a big fuss about it, so when you and I dined there she wanted to impress you by serving you the same Niagara-on-the-Lake wine as you had there before. She will also testify at your trial that you asked for your steak bones to be bagged because you had left the dog in the car while you went in for dinner." concluded Dave.

"These charges are ridiculous." said Ken.

Just then, Dave Alexander, usually a calm collected professional police officer catapults from his chair and lands himself directly in front of Stratten. He removed his service revolver from the holster under his suit jacket. He raises the gun and pushes the delivery end of the barrel firmly into the forehead of Ken Stratten.

"Give me one reason I shouldn't shoot you right now?" he asks.

A nervous hesitation exists in the room. No one makes a move or a sound.

"Because Dave, then you'd be just like me wouldn't you?" Ken says.

"Dr. Ken Stratten," said Chief Ronalds, "You are under arrest for the murders of Angela and Jimmy Benson."

Ken is removed by uniformed police officers who had been summoned by the Chief.

Several minutes of silence in the room allows everyone's heart rates to return to near normal.

"Anyone care for dinner?" Dave asks, "I know a great place for steaks and wine."

Not unexpected, there were no takers.

The End

Buffalo New York Police Officer Dave Alexander joins romantic and tactical forces with his Scottish counterpart Constable Janet Angus in my next book entitled "DRIP."

Printed in the United States
54529LVS00001B/268-288

9 781424 129775